SMALL TOWN LIES CAN BE DEADLY

THE

LIES

BETWEEN

US

INTERNATIONAL BESTSELLING AUTHOR
YOLANDA OLSON

ACKNOWLEDGMENTS

To my team of wonderful PAs, Lis, Linda, and Dawn, thank you for sitting through the headache that is Yolanda Olson and not quitting on me. You ladies are the rocks that hold me up when I want to toss books into the fire.

Abigail Davies of Pink Elephant Designs for a cover I knew I just had to have as soon as I saw it! Thank you for bringing beauty into the light where a tragedy lies in wake.

Evelyn Summers of Pinpoint Editing, for coming through in a clutch! Your work is always appreciated!

To my wonderful readers who allow me to keep doing this: hold on tight. This is a wild one.

Prologue

Sing Sing Correctional Facility

The air in the hallway is thick with sweat. The guard smells of stale cigarettes and rank pussy, but this is a men's prison, so he obviously didn't think a shower would have been in order before starting his shift today. He sucks his teeth as he walks, and scratches his oversized gut. His sickly blue shirt is hugging him tightly, the buttons clinging to the fabric for dear life, and he keeps pulling up his black pants.

He looks over and smiles down at me for what seems like the hundredth time. He's missing a few teeth here and there, which makes me wonder how much he paid his hooker for a fuck back at his place.

"You must be someone special, kid. He usually declines visits from everyone," the guard says as he unclips a large ring of keys from his belt. I raise an eyebrow at the gold ring around the third finger on his left hand and then back up at him.

Maybe he's nice?

I'm clearly in no position to judge someone based on how they look or act, but I can't help it. Being judgmental has gotten me this far in life, and I think I've been doing okay for myself—not that I've been given a choice.

However, I refuse to let the past hold me back. I owe it to myself to be better than the steaming pile of shit life has tried to bestow upon me.

And that's why I'm here.

I can't move forward without all my questions answered, and I'm not entirely sure he'll be willing to tell me what I want to know.

"I guess so," I reply softly.

The guard sucks his teeth again as he fiddles

with the keys until he finds the right one to unlock the gate. It's a sound I'll have nightmares about, if it doesn't drive me mad first.

He finally pulls the white, steel gate open and motions for me to step in. I nod at another guard who's heading our way. He smiles at me and returns my nod as I wait patiently for the next leg of the walk.

"What's your name, kid?" he asks me, as he continues down the long hallway.

I look up at him with sad eyes and shake my head slightly. I know his curiosity is meant to be a small kindness, but I don't want to get too personal right now. If I get all the answers that I've come for, I won't need to come back again.

"Ah, that's alright," he says with an understanding nod. "We're almost there anyway. My name is Officer Davis, and if you need anything from me, you just call out my name, ya hear? I'll come over and help you out if shit gets to be too much."

"Thank you," I reply, my voice barely above a whisper.

He nods again, and we continue the rest of the walk in silence. One more heavy steel gate, one more jingle of the keys, before we finally reach our destination. A small room with only a single, clear pane of glass sitting between two chairs and two wired phones. I glance up and see a camera, its red light watching me, careful to record my every move.

"They're bringing him up now. Do you want me to stay with you? I'm not really supposed to, but I can if you want me to."

"I'll be okay," I reply, sitting down in the chair.

Liar.

"Alright," he says with a nod. "Remember; if this gets to be too much, you knock on this door and yell 'Officer Davis', and I'll come in and break it up, okay?"

I glance up at him and smile weakly as he turns and walks out. The palms of my hands are sweating, and I quickly wipe them on my jeans as I glance up at the camera again.

Then, I hear him—his laughter, his casually loud voice, as he jokes with the corrections officer who's bringing him to the room. It's been over a decade since I've seen him, and I'm not quite sure if he'll look the same. He's been here for the past fifteen years, waiting for the needle—an eye for an eye. We live in one of the states where if you take a life, your life will balance the cost of the transgression.

I become rigid as the door opens and the officer enters first, a smile on his face. I can tell that he genuinely enjoys his company, and I can understand that, because once upon a time, I did too. I thought he was the greatest man who ever walked the face of the earth, and to be honest, he really is.

I drop my eyes to my hands as I hear the chains rattling. He's walking into the room now, and his laughter has subsided. The officer with him gives us both some rules, and even though neither of us are listening, I mumble a meager "okay" just to get him to leave.

He sits in his chair—I know it, because I can hear it creak under the weight of his body—and picks up his phone. My lower lip trembling, I reach for mine and place it to my ear, before I finally look up at him.

Ten years changes a man, but not this one—not much. The last I had seen of him was a picture he sent me five years ago when he finally responded to my letters. He still looks similar to the man I remember, except now he's got some gray streaks in his shorn beard, as well as some white showing evenly on the sides of his short, black hair. He seems bigger than when I last saw him. He's always been a solid man, yet I don't recall him being *this* steadily built. I can tell he doesn't have much to do behind these walls, and he seems to pass the time by spending his days in the gym.

But his eyes. Oh, his eyes are still the same. Cold, hard, and the most beautiful light brown color I've ever seen, like my favorite milk chocolate candy bars he would give me when Momma wasn't looking.

Our secret, baby girl. You know how she gets with sweets, he would say each time. Hoyt Blackburn always knew how to keep a secret or two in his day. He made damn sure I was just as good as being tight-lipped about some of the things he did that I'd stumble onto by accident from time to time. And the easiest way to keep a little girl quiet was to give her her favorite piece of candy.

Sweet like a piece of candy. I've heard that little phrase uttered enough times as a child, I think with a slight shudder.

But here we are after ten long years, face to face again, and perhaps for the last time.

Hoyt's staring at me with a curiosity and warmth that makes me tremble slightly. However, I do my best to push my fear away, because I want to get my questions answered before they put this dog to rest, and that's what I intend to do.

"Hi, Daddy."

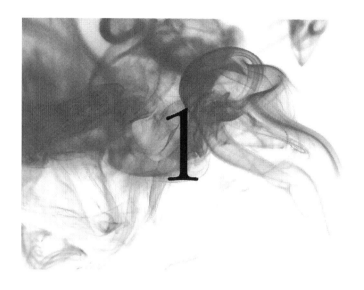

1

It's roughly an eight hour drive back home, with a couple of stops here and there for gas and to stretch my legs. I've been gone for seventy-two hours, and I know I'll be going to an empty bed when I arrive, because my other half hates being in our place alone. He's told me countless times that it's hard for him to sleep in a bed without me lying next to him these days, and I can understand that, since I'm the same way.

It'll make these long trips easier for me, though. I tried to sleep in a hotel when I arrived in Ossining, and when that didn't settle well with me, I tried to sleep in my car. After that, I decided that short naps would have to do until I was back in my bed where I belonged.

He's gonna be so pissed when he finds out where I've been.

Jori Davidson is the only man, besides Daddy, that I've ever honestly, truly loved. He's been by my side for as long as I can remember, always there to wipe the tears away and tell me things would get better one day. When things went to shit with Momma and Daddy, he would sneak me out of my bedroom window, and we'd hide out in his backyard tree house. We spent plenty of nights soaked in my tears and wallowing in my pity, and he never left my side or told me I was overreacting.

You don't forget things like that, no matter how hard the storm is crashing all around you.

I always felt bad for him, though, 'cause no matter how hard it started to get with Momma and Daddy arguing more often than not, at least I had them. Jori was raised by his aunt and uncle, 'cause his parents wanted nothing to do with him.

A bad seed, they called him. Even at such a young age, they thought he would never amount to much, and so they decided it would be best to get rid of him.

I rub my eyes tiredly as I finally see a sign for Harpers Ferry. Another hundred more miles or so, and I'll be able to get a solid, good night's sleep.

I lean over slightly toward the passenger seat and feel around for my phone. The battery is full again, so I pull it free from the charging chord carefully, and hold it up to eye level.

I sigh heavily after bringing the screen to life. Jori still hasn't responded to any of my text messages, though he's called me a handful of times since Thursday night, but not in the past twenty-four hours. He has attachment issues, and I get it; being rejected by almost everyone who's supposed to care about you when you're so damn young will do that to a person, but I've never given him a reason not to trust me.

It's just that I'm so used to keeping secrets when it comes to Hoyt—even from Jori. I toss my phone back onto the seat and reach for the visor. I keep my cigarettes hidden there, because he doesn't like it when I smoke, but it'll help me stay awake for the rest of the drive.

I'm kinda proud of myself. I've gone from a pack a day to half a pack, and I'm pretty sure I'll be done smoking completely as soon as the State of New York executes Hoyt. Not that I want him to die, though, because I believe everyone deserves a second chance, and I think that's why I went out to see him after so long.

I've been following his story on the *Ossining Daily Voice* website. His lawyers have filed appeal after appeal, but it doesn't seem like he's had much say in the matters going on. That's just how he's always been, though—carefree about life, even when it's his own that hangs in the balance.

I can't ever remember Hoyt raising a hand to me in anger as a child. Come to think of it, he never hit any of us; not even Momma. He just raised his voice with her when he was angry, and it was like listening to thunder split the sky. Usually, it was enough to get her to shut up, and she would take a swipe at him a time or two. Even then, the most he would do was push her away to protect her from what we all knew he could do to her.

Hoyt isn't all bad. At least, he tried not to be, and in a weird way, even though I don't know him like I used to, it kinda breaks my heart that he's on death row.

The rest of the drive goes by in a haze of loud rock music and two cigarettes smoked to the butt.

The wind whipping through the window tousles my long, cherry red hair around my face, and keeps me in good spirits.

The one thing I got from Hoyt was his soul-crushing eyes, but the hair and spitfire temper, I got from Momma.

I let out a sigh of relief when my street finally comes into view. One of my headlights blew out somewhere in Baltimore, and I chalk it up the little bit of Blackburn luck I still have working for me that I hadn't been pulled over.

Cops aren't really out at this time of night, anyway. Most of them that I know are too busy making a false arrest on prostitutes so they can get free blow jobs, and then letting them go with stern warnings of staying off the street.

Until the next time. 'Cause Lord knows that there's always a next time.

At the end of the road is where I live. It's ironic, now that I think about it. I ran far away from home when the chance was presented, and I moved to the end of a road in a sleepy town. In a way, me and Hoyt have found ourselves in the same place—even if he doesn't know it yet.

I pull into my driveway and turn off the car, take the keys out of the ignition, and sigh, pushing my hair back out of my face. Reaching over, I grab my phone from the seat and scoop my purse off the floor where it fell. If anything spilled out of it, I'll worry about it tomorrow. I just want my fucking bed right now.

As soon as I step out of my car and close the door, I almost scream. I wasn't expecting any visitors tonight, but there he is, sitting on the back step, head in his hands, and shaking his leg.

Fuck.

"Where ya been, Red?"

Jori's called me that since we were little. From the first time he asked me what my name was and I told him, he said that he thought my hair was prettier than my name, so he decided right then and there to call me Red.

"Gracie? But that's a girl's name," he complained with a scrunched up look on his little boy face. I remember laughing at how appalled he seemed, and agreed that Red was much better than what I had been given.

"Hey, Jori," I greet him as brightly as I can in my tired state. He won't be very happy if he knows I've been visiting with Hoyt, because to him, Hoyt is the dragon he'd had stormed the castle to save me from.

A dragon recognizes their own kind, I reason to myself as I pull the strap of my purse up over my shoulder.

He looks up at me with his bitter blue eyes and red face. He's been crying, he's been angry, and now he's relieved, but for how long? He gets to his feet and shoves his hands into his pockets. The way he's standing right now reminds me of the young, angry boy I first met, and I can't help but smile.

"I left on Thursday when you didn't come home, you know? But I've been by every single day and night since then, and you weren't here. You haven't been answering my phone calls … Have you been stepping out on me?" he asks. His words are rushed and rambling, which tells me he doesn't know what to believe, nor did he want to believe the worst, but he'll accept whatever I tell him.

"No."

"So where the fuck have you been?" he asks angrily. He takes a deep breath and looks away from me. Jori never liked to raise his voice to me, and is always quick to apologize, but the pain he feels in his heart must be unbearable since I've been away from him.

Four days. It's the longest we've been apart

since it all happened, and I left him without a word as to where I was going.

"Ossining," I reply quietly.

"What?" he asks in confusion. "Where is that?"

"New York," I say with a heavy sigh. I walk over to him and pull his hands out of his pockets, pulling him behind me as I sit down on the back step. "Sing Sing, to be exact."

"The prison?" he questions, pulling one of his hands away from me to clean his face of errant tears. "Why?"

"Why do you think?" I ask him quietly, giving him a forlorn smile. Jori raises an eyebrow at me before the look of understanding washes over his face. He chuckles and shakes his head, as he reaches over and puts an arm around my shoulders.

Jori Davidson has what I call a sexy serial killer look to him. His eyes, while absolutely bitter and intense, can pierce the heart in whatever way he chooses. He's got a couple of large tattoos on either side of his neck, and his arms are covered down to the hands. His hair is black like Hoyt's, but his is a bit longer, and I think that's secretly part of the reason I like being around him so much.

In the oddest of ways, he reminds me of what I lost. Even though he's tall, slender and solid unlike Hoyt, he's an ever looming presence of comfort and hope in a world gone to shit in the blink of an eye.

"Did you see him?" he asks me quietly.

I nod and lean my head on his shoulder. And for the first time in a very long time, I feel tears slowly begin to roll down my face. I hadn't cried for Hoyt since they first arrested him. Hell, I was even indifferent when he got the death penalty, because I knew it wouldn't make a difference in the world to him either way, but having seen him again after so long ... seeing that smile on his face and feeling his eyes on me again after ten long years seems to have struck a chord inside me—one I thought I had long since severed.

"And how's the old man doing?"

I shrug and gently rub my face on his shirt. I didn't realize how much I missed the way Jori smelled until now. An intoxicating mix of pine and wintergreen that always helps put me to sleep with ease on the nights when the dreams take over and attempt to torment me into staying awake.

"You don't wanna talk about it?" he asks, brushing his lips against my forehead.

"No," I reply quietly.

Jori nods and gets to his feet. "Okay. You don't have to, not tonight, but I'd like to know what happened eventually, okay?"

I look up at him and smile, nodding in silent agreement.

"I'm gonna get going, now I know you're okay and that I haven't been replaced," he says with a nervous laugh as he fishes around in his pocket for his keys.

"What?"

It honestly shocks me that he's been casing the place for days, and now that I'm finally home again, he's intent on leaving.

"You need your rest, Red. If I stay here tonight, neither of us is gonna get much sleep. It's okay, I'll go crash at Aunt Millie's house; it's where I've been staying the past few days, anyway," he says with a laugh.

"Get your ass in this house," I reply, getting to my feet and reaching into my purse for the house keys. "I've barely slept as it is, and I'd like to get at least one full night before I have to worry about when I'll be seeing you again."

Jori chuckles and wraps his arms around my

waist as I fiddle with the lock. He places a gentle kiss on the back of my neck, and I smile.

"You get the couch tonight, buddy," I say playfully. "I actually plan on getting some sleep."

Jori gives my ass a playful slap once I get the door open as he follows me inside. Tossing my purse onto the small table by the door, I take a deep breath and smile.

"I promise I'll sleep on the couch once you're out cold, Red. We both know it'll be easier for the both of us if we hang out in bed until then," he says as he follows me back to the bedroom.

I push the door open and crawl into bed. I didn't think I was actually as tired as I am, until Jori puts an arm around my waist, kisses the side of my head, and holds me close.

Maybe it's the magic of being in his arms again; maybe it's the simple comfort of being in my own bed. Either way, I yawn loudly and close my eyes.

Life might not be perfect, but for right now, it's not so bad. I'll worry about tomorrow when it comes, because that's when I'll have to tell Jori that I'll be going back to see Hoyt, and attempt to keep the secrets from him just a little while longer.

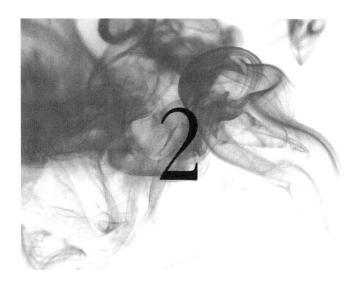

2

Things always feel different when the sun rises in your own bedroom window. Somehow, it's not as foreboding when you're in a place you don't know, unaware of what the day's events will bring. I stretch and roll onto my side, smiling when I hear the television on in the living room. I half expected him to leave because I'd banished him to the couch, but I guess he missed me as much as I missed him, otherwise I would have woken up to a quiet, empty home.

I don't want to get out of bed just yet, but I also don't want to leave Jori alone longer than he needs to be. I push myself up to a seated position and let my feet dangle for a moment. I'm not exactly tall, which is something else I got from Momma, and Jori actually seems to like it a lot, so I tend not to let it bother me.

Rubbing my eyes tiredly, I hop off the bed and head toward the bathroom. A morning piss, a good scrub of the teeth, and I'll head into the living room to find out what he's doing.

After using the toilet and washing my hands, I begin to brush my teeth and giggle when I hear his raucous laughter coming from the other room. He sounds something like a sick hyena when he laughs, and I think it's the best fucking thing I've ever heard in my entire life.

Besides *"sweet like a piece of candy"*, anyway. It turns my stomach and excites me at the same time, and I've never fully understood why. How those two emotions could possibly come together so fluidly is beyond me, but they do, whenever I think about Hoyt whispering those words.

I lean into the mirror and inspect my teeth once I'm done, before drying my hands on the small hand towel I keep neatly folded next to the sink, and walk out when I'm satisfied that I'm as presentable as I can be right now.

"Morning," I say with a yawn as I enter the living room.

"Afternoon," he corrects, as he turns his head to look at me. He's lying on the couch with one arm folded behind his head, no shirt, and a pair of gym shorts. I always find him to be sexiest when he's comfortable and lounging around, because it's when he's the most relaxed, and Jori can be very tightly wound at times.

"Wow, I didn't think I'd be asleep that long. Sorry about that," I say, walking over to the couch and picking up his legs. Once I sit down, I let them rest on my lap and sigh.

I know I have to prepare myself for the inevitable flurry of questions that I know will be coming at some point. Jori senses my lack of comfort at the moment, because he reaches forward and takes my hand in his, giving it a squeeze as he goes back to the movie he's watching.

I raise an eyebrow when I realize he's watching *The Texas Chainsaw Massacre* for what seems like the one billionth time. It's his favorite movie, and I get why he was laughing now; he absolutely adores the weird family in the film.

I glance at him in amusement when the girl tied

up in the attic wakes up. He loves the way the brother mocks her, and it sends him off into another fit of laughter, which makes me giggle in return.

"Don't you ever get sick of this movie?" I ask, rubbing his shin with my free hand.

"Nah; it's great family fun," he remarks with a sly grin. I roll my eyes and smile. Jori doesn't let the fact that his parents didn't want him ever weigh on his head, and that's something I admire.

It's better to not be wanted than wanted *too* much, I think. Especially not in the way that most children are—cruel and unnerving ways can damage a person more than not wanting them at all.

A shudder ripples through me, causing Jori to swing his legs off of my lap, and he wraps an arm around my shoulder, pulling me close. Being in his arms is really the equivalent of a security blanket, and he always knows when I need it. I let out a sigh and rest my head on his shoulder as we watch the rest of the movie. A few more gleeful cackles from him, a maniac with a chainsaw dancing in the sunrise, and a bloodied girl screaming in terror as she's driven away from him later, and the credits are rolling.

"You hungry, yet?" he asks, letting go of me and walking over to the entertainment center to turn off the PlayStation and television.

"Not really," I reply honestly.

"Good. I wanted to go out for dinner anyway, which means we've got some time to kill."

He turns and grins at me deviously. I smile, shake my head, and hold up my hands in surrender, to which the light leaves his eyes slightly, and he shrugs.

"It was worth a shot," he replies, the grin not leaving his handsome face, as he lies back down on the couch and drapes his legs over me again.

I run my fingers down the colorful designs that adorn his leg, but think better of my actions when he shifts. Out of the corner of my eye, I can see that this simple touch is already affecting him, and I'm really not in the mood to fuck right now.

"I'm gonna take a shower. Think of where you wanna go to eat, and don't do the girl thing, please. Actually figure out where you want to go, okay?" he says as he leans up and kisses me quickly on the lips, before leaving me in the living room alone.

I take a deep breath, smile happily, and rub my arms. I don't know how I got lucky enough to end up with a guy like Jori; he's seen me at my worst, yet never at my best, and he still doesn't leave me. All he ever asks for is honesty and affection—the very things he was denied as a child.

I get up from the couch and pick up his jeans and t-shirt from the carpet. I decide I'll leave them outside the bathroom so he runs right into them and remembers not to do the "guy" thing. Jori doesn't have many faults, but he's all man when it comes to leaving his damn clothes and socks around.

I can hear him singing to himself in the shower as I neatly fold his clothes and leave them directly outside the door, then head back to the bedroom. Since dinner isn't for a few hours, I think a nap may be in order until then. Yet as soon as I lay my head down on my pillows, I feel guilty for wanting to sleep some more when I haven't seen him in so long.

He'll understand, I think as I yawn and roll onto my side. I close my eyes and reach down for my sheets blindly, pulling them up to my neck and nestling deeper into the mattress. I'll make it up to him after we get back from dinner, and everything will be okay. The sun will still set, the moon will still rise, and I'll still have to find a way to tell him that I'm going back to Ossining next week; all of the wonderful and terribly inevitable things that will have to fall into place before the night is over.

"Hey, Red?"

I'm roused from my half sleep by Jori calling for me. I sigh and roll onto my back. I didn't even realize I was falling asleep until I had been woken up.

"Yes?" I call out groggily.

"Come here for a sec please?" he calls back.

I let out my breath in a huff as I push myself off the bed and walk slowly toward the bathroom, rubbing my eyes. I hope he's not expecting me to put his clothes in his hamper for him—not that he's incapable of it, he just likes act like a Neanderthal sometimes, thinking it's cuter than it really is.

"What's up?" I ask curiously as I enter the bathroom. He's leaning over the sink, looking into the mirror, with only a white towel around his waist, and I can't help but appreciate his finely toned body.

"Do you see this?" he asks, leaning closer to the mirror.

"See what?" I inquire as I stop next to him and lean into the mirror to see what he's looking at.

"This," he says again softly, as he turns around

and puts his hands on my hips, and lifts me onto the edge of the sink. I should have known it was a ruse, but when he kisses me deeply, with a hunger he hasn't bared in so long, I immediately forgive the deception.

I run my hands back through his hair and pull him closer to me. The heat of his freshly washed body against mine is fucking intoxicating, and I want nothing more than to be drunk on him, but I know it has to wait until we talk about Hoyt.

"Ease up there, big fella," I whisper with a chuckle as I place my hands on his chest, and push him away slightly.

Jori lets out a groan as he places his forehead against mine. "Come *on*, Red," he complains.

"Don't be mad at me. I just … I think it'll be better to wait until we have dinner and I can tell you about my trip, okay?"

He pulls back, taking my face in his hands, and looks into my eyes. Jori's are so fucking serious, and a little unnerving, but he finally nods, kisses my forehead, and lets me hop off the sink.

"This better be some fucking story you have to tell me," he mutters, just as I make it to the door. I turn around and glance at him to find him leaning over the sink again, staring down at the ceramic, before he shakes his head and opens the medicine cabinet.

Even though he's no longer interested in my presence, I still nod before going back to the bedroom. Jori doesn't like secrets, because he says there's nothing we shouldn't be able to tell each other.

If only that were true, I think as I climb back into my bed, pull the sheets up again, and close my eyes.

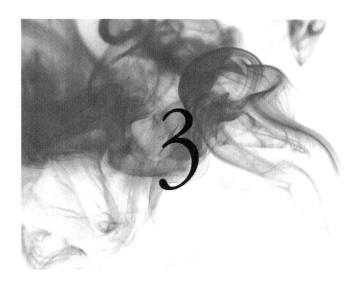

3

The sun was setting when I woke up. I decided to run into the bathroom and take a quick shower, enough to wash the sweat off and clean myself up as best as I could, then ran out to the car where Jori was patiently waiting.

"You look pretty," he says, smiling at me.

"Thank you," I respond with a shy smile, as I pull the seatbelt across my shoulder and buckle it into place. I push my hair behind my ears and wait patiently as he turns the car on. I'm curious as to why he's being so friendly right now, considering I shot him down a little while ago, but I'm sure that will come to light soon enough.

"So, where are we dining tonight, my lady?" he asks in an over-exaggerated, gentlemanly tone.

"Um, wanna go to The Anvil?" I ask, giving a peculiar look. That tone swap caught me off guard, and I hope he doesn't plan on doing that again anytime soon.

"Sure, if that's what you're in the mood for, then let's do it," he replies, as he checks the side-view mirror before pulling out into the street.

Once we're on the road, he reaches over and takes my hand, lacing his fingers with mine. For the most part, it's a quiet, short drive, which I appreciate, since I'll be fielding more questions than I care for soon enough.

Jori finds a spot on the street a few spots down from the front door, and parks. As he turns the car off, he leans over and kisses me on the cheek, then gets out and walks over to my side of the car. I roll my eyes and laugh as I undo my seat-belt and wait for him to open the door. He may have changed his tone up to some weird *Jeeves* thing earlier, but he really can be a gentleman when he wants to be.

He presses the button on the key remote to

lock and arm the car, then takes my hand and leads me toward the rustic little restaurant I love so much. Jori opens the door to the place and holds it for me so I can walk in, then steps in behind me, wrapping his arms around my waist and placing his head on my shoulder.

We approach the little podium with a "please wait to be seated sign" next to it, and he nuzzles my neck gently.

"Mm. You smell good, Red," he says softly, as he breathes me in. I've never let anyone get this close to me before—not willingly, anyway, but I know Jori's different. He's never hurt me before, and I know he never will, because he's too busy playing the knight in tattooed armor role in my life.

Even with the dragon almost slain, he acts like he still has to protect me from the world.

"Hello!" a young woman greets us cheerfully. I jump at the sound of her voice and sudden appearance, causing Jori to chuckle. His hands leave my waist as he moves toward the podium, crosses his arms over the mantel, leans in, and smiles at her.

"Two please," he says with a sly grin and a sparkle in his eyes. "Gotta feed her before I can fuck her, you know?"

"Jori!" I exclaim, playfully slapping him on the back. The young girl's face turns a slight shade of crimson, but who wouldn't with someone as charming and sexy as Jori Davidson a few mere feet from their face?

She grabs two menus and tells us to follow her. I poke him in the ribs as soon as she turns her back to us, and he rolls his eyes.

"It was just a joke, Red. Sorry," he mumbles, falling into step beside me.

"Not to me," I say to him softly.

Letting out a sigh, he nods, and as we reach a little booth in the back corner, I slide in and look up at him expectantly.

"Hey. Um. I'm sorry about what I said up there," Jori says to the young woman, nodding toward the podium. "It was rude and I wanted to apologize."

She smiles at him and nods, placing a menu down in front of me as he slides into the spot next to him. Once his menu is handed to him, she lets us know that our server will be with us shortly.

"Thank you," I say, turning as much as I can to face him. "I know that was hard for you."

"No problem," he says, widening his eyes for a brief moment and chewing on his lower lip. "What looks good?"

Jori may be damn good at a lot of things that matter to me, but apologizing is just not one of them. He says it takes him a lot to swallow his pride and say he's sorry, and because of that, he's usually much more careful not to do things to be sorry for.

"Besides you?" I ask, giving him a playful nudge. He lets out a short laugh as he flips the menu back over, opens it, and begins to look over the selections.

"Seriously though, Red. What are you hungry for?" he asks, reaching over and opening my menu. "Besides me, of course."

I smirk as he steals a glance out of the corner of his eye, then lean my head on his shoulder as I look at the choices. The words and pictures are blurring, because the truth is, I'm not really hungry. The worry I'm feeling from telling him about my visit with Hoyt is enough to fill any hunger inside me for the time being.

"Hi, there!" another young girl greets us. She's got short-cropped brown hair, a piercing in her lip, and friendly hazel colored eyes. "My name is Elizabeth, and I'll be taking care of you guys this evening. Can I start you off with something to drink?"

"I'll have some apple juice," I say, glancing up at her from the comfort of Jori's shoulder. He turns his head slightly down at me and asks if it's okay if he has a beer, and I nod. One beer won't render him useless when it comes to driving us back, and it might actually help keep him calm once the story starts to flow out of me.

Jori orders his beer, closes his menu, and slips an arm around my shoulders. I still haven't decided what I want to eat yet, but I guess an appetizer will have to do. It'll hurt his manhood that I'm not ordering some big meal, 'cause he always thinks he doesn't have enough money to support us, but I don't need much, and I've told him that a thousand times over.

Elizabeth returns a few moments later and places our drinks in front of us, before pulling out her order pad and a pen from her apron.

"Alright; what can I get for you guys?" she asks with a friendly smile and her pen poised over the pad.

"I'll take the seared ribeye and some of those amazing garlic mashed potatoes I know you've got hiding back there somewhere," he says, handing her his menu. She nods as she writes down his order and asks him how he wants his meat cooked. "Medium-well is just fine with me."

"And for you?" she asks, writing down his directions, then glancing up at me.

"Um, I'll take the tortilla chips and salsa dip, please," I say, passing Jori my menu. He's giving me a disappointed look, but I'm being very careful to ignore it without hurting his feelings too much.

He waits for Elizabeth to walk away before he turns to look at me. "Really? That's all you're having?"

"I'm just not very hungry," I reply with a shrug. "I think I'm topped off on all the snacks I had on the road still. Nothing more, nothing less."

He lets out a heavy sigh and runs his hand back through his hair. He's using his "I'm pissed off, but we're in public, so I won't make a scene" trademark move, and I decide to shrug out from beneath his arm.

I don't want to argue with Jori, but he's not the one who has to deal with the shit I have to. He sees everything from the outside, and somehow thinks that makes him a martyr for whatever fucking cause he thinks I have.

It doesn't.

There is no martyrdom to be had here, and soon, there won't even be any more dragons to slay, and with as much as I love him, I'm not sure I'll really need him anymore.

When Hoyt dies, a big piece of me will too, and I'm afraid that the part of me that loves Jori will be buried with him. Maybe I'm worrying for nothing, maybe I'm not, but I guess it's true what they say—time will tell.

"Come on, don't do that," he says quietly as he rests a hand on my thigh. "I'm sorry I get shitty when it comes to stuff like this, but I wanted tonight to be special, you know? We haven't seen each other in a while, and I wanted you to have anything you wanted."

"I'll have what I want when those chips come out here," I reply, turning my head and leaning up to glance over the seat. "Who knows? Maybe I'll steal some of your food when you're not looking, too."

Jori laughs, this time a good-natured laugh, and I turn back around and smile at him. When he's genuinely happy, his smile can light up the fucking world. You can see eternity in his eyes, and everything seems like it'll be okay, even if just for the moment we're in.

"Hey, can I ask you something?" I inquire, leaning forward and placing my elbow on the table. I let my chin fall into my hand as he takes a sip of his beer and nods. "What do I smell like to you?"

He raises a curious eyebrow at me as he sets his glass down and smiles, "What?"

"Well, just a little while ago, you said I smell good. I'm curious about what I smell like to you," I reply, tilting my head and grinning.

"Hm, well," he says, leaning back and drumming his fingers on the table. He moves quickly toward me, taking in a whiff, before falling back against the seat, smiling. Jori cuts his eyes playfully toward me and I grin at him expectantly. "Fresh hyacinth on a warm spring day."

My face flushes red and Jori grins. I don't know if he's telling me the truth so much as probably reciting the can of air freshener we keep in the house, but I'll take it.

Before either of us can say anything else, Elizabeth reappears with our plates of food on a large tray.

"Um, would you mind sitting on the other side while we eat?" I ask him with a nervous smile.

Jori raises an eyebrow at me and gives me a

confused smile, but nods and slides out of the booth, repositioning himself across from me. He shakes his head as he pulls his jacket off and thanks Elizabeth when she sets his plate in front of him.

"Can I have another beer when you get a chance?" he asks her, opening up his napkin and tossing it aside for now.

"Sure can!" she replies with a nod, setting my plate of chips and salsa down. "Would you like a top off there?"

I shake my head and she nods, "Be right back with your beer."

He clears his throat as he picks up his fork and knife, cuts off a piece of his steak, and shoves it in his mouth. He gives me a big smile as he chews his food, and I'm wondering how long it'll take him to just hand over the keys without my asking him to.

I shake my head slightly and lean forward, picking up a chip, and dipping it into the salsa. It's a little spicy for my liking, but actually tastes pretty good. Elizabeth returns, and as she places Jori's beer down, she asks us how everything is. I nod politely and he tells her we're okay for now, as he takes a huge swig of his drink. She retrieves the half empty glass from the table and walks away with it.

"Shout if you need anything!" she calls out cheerfully as she disappears into the kitchen.

We eat in silence for a little while, with only playful little actions keeping us aware of each other's company. I lean over a few times to try to steal some of Jori's mashed potatoes with a tortilla chip, continuously failing when he raises his fork to fend me off.

It makes us both laugh, and eventually he holds up a forkful of his potatoes to me and slides it through my now parted lips. I laugh and slap his hand away when he begins to slowly move the fork in and out of my mouth, a look of delightful seduction in his eyes.

"Well damn, why'd you stop?" he asks with a wicked grin.

"Because I'm not here to blow the utensils?" I quip with a laugh.

"Hm. Fair enough," he says, placing his fork down and leaning on the table with his elbows. He picks up his glass of beer and maintains eye contact with me as he begins to drink what's left of it.

Here it comes, I think as the smile starts to leave my face.

"I'm gonna go take a leak, flag that girl down

and get me another beer, and then I wanna hear all about your little adventure," he says in a quiet tone, getting up from the booth and walking away without so much as a backward glance.

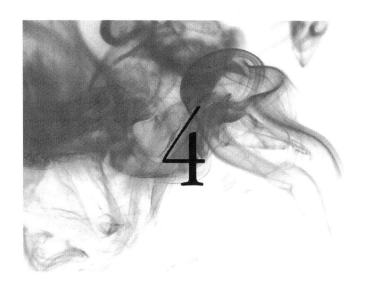

Cold Spring, NY 1994

"Millie's gonna be so pissed that I took her car," Jori says with a laugh as he accelerates down the street.

"I think she'll be even more pissed if you get us killed!" I squeal, pushing my hands against the roof as he barrels around a corner.

"Yeah, yeah," he replies with a grin as he relents on the gas. I giggle and check my seat-belt to make sure it's securely in place, and lean my head out of the window, letting it whip my hair around freely.

The car stops at a red light and he lets go of the wheel, running his hands back through his hair.

"Where do you wanna go? Anywhere in particular?"

I look at him, purse my lips, and shake my head. The place never matters when I've got my best friend with me. It's his company that makes the days more tolerable since Daddy got arrested. It's been five years since he was tried and convicted of killing Momma. They gave him death, and he gave no fucks when the judge asked him if he had anything to say.

Well, that's not entirely true. He did get up to the podium and tell me that he'll always love me and that I should remember the way we were, and not how things became. I cried a lot that day, because the only parent that actually gave a shit about me was being taken away from me.

Jori's been by side since before it happened, and he promised me he'd never leave me, no matter what. He's kept true to his word, and comes over to Uncle Jake's house as often as he can. I don't know why I was sent to live with Momma's brother, but he's nice to me and doesn't treat me like I'm an inconvenience.

"Hey, wanna go to Canada?" he asks, breaking into my thoughts.

"What? We don't have passports; they'll never let us in," I reply with a laugh.

"Maybe, maybe not. We won't know unless we try," he says with a smirk and a wiggle of his eyebrows.

"You are absolutely insane, Jori Davidson," I respond, still laughing.

"And *you* have no sense of adventure, Red. Come on; it'll be fun!" he pleads, his eyes lighting up with excitement.

I tilt my head at him and realize how serious he is about this. The car behind us lays on the horn and he leans an arm out the window with his middle finger in the air. We may be just "a couple of crazy kids" like Uncle Jake tends to call us, but goddamn, he acts like more of an adult than most I've ever come across.

"Babe, it's our song!" he says excitedly, raising the volume up on the radio. The chords for *Interstate Love Song* start coming through the speakers, and that's when I make up my mind.

"Guess that means we should head to Canada then," I say, grinning at him.

"Fucking right!" he whoops happily as he turns

the car around and heads toward the freeway, cutting off the oncoming traffic. Jori reaches down and takes my hand in his, and kisses the top of it happily as he guns it toward the on ramp. I'm not sure how long it'll take us to get there, and if we have enough money between us to make it, but that will just have to be part of the adventure.

The song keeps blaring out of the speaker and he begins to sing happily along, squeezing my hand each time the chorus comes on.

It's strange how something as simple as stealing his aunt's car and running away from Uncle Jake can make me feel so alive.

Millie's yelled at me a few times when she's found us hanging out together in the basement of her house where he stays. Jori managed to turn it into a rec room over the years, and it's an absolute dream down there, but she doesn't like me being near him.

The last time I was there was right after Daddy got arrested,, and she told me I'm good for nothing like Momma, and that it's no wonder he treated her the way he did.

That made Jori explode. I've never seen him as angry as he was that day, and he warned her that if she ever spoke to me like that again, he'd make her sorry she even opened her mouth to begin with. I remember how scared she looked when he said that; she retreated right back up the stairs with her tail tucked firmly between her legs, and he held me in his arms while I cried.

I don't know what kind of person says that to a nine year old kid, but she never did mention it again after Jori put her in her place. When I was done crying that day, I couldn't help but admire how much fear an angry twelve year old could put into an adult, but we weren't doing anything wrong. We would just spend our time watching television and hanging out.

"She's a fucking, useless cow," he'd said to me while I wailed into his chest. "Don't let her bother you, Red. You'll always have me, I promise."

"Aren't you worried that Millie's gonna report the car stolen?" I suddenly ask him. She's definitely vindictive enough to do it, and knowing her, she'd toss in a bullshit lie about him kidnapping me just to keep us apart.

"Not if she knows what's good for her," he remarks casually as he adjusts the rear-view mirror slightly and smiles quickly at me.

Five years, and nothing has changed. Jori's gotten older, angrier, and if at all possible, even more bitter than he was before, yet he always manages to find a way to keep that in check when he's with me. There hasn't been one time I can think of that he's so much as raised his voice to me, so I can only imagine how Millie manages to sleep at night, knowing what's downstairs waiting for her if she crosses one line too many.

About an hour into our trip, Jori decides to pull off the highway to get some gas and use the restroom. As we walk into the gas station convenience store, he takes my hand and keeps me close to him.

"Hey, can I get twenty dollars on that pump over there?" he asks the clerk, nodding toward Millie's car.

"Sure," the man replies with a pleasant nod. "Just come back in and get your change, 'cause I doubt that's gonna take twenty dollars to fill up, son."

Jori looks up at him for a moment and scoffs as he continues to peel one dollar bills out of his wallet and slide them across the counter toward him. I know being called "son" is what got that reaction of out him. He's not used to anyone calling him that, and I can tell it bothered him a little bit.

"I'm gonna go take a leak. Here," he says, holding his wallet out to me, "grab us some sodas and a few bags of chips, and I'll meet you outside."

I smile up at him and reach into my bra, pulling out a small, folded stack of twenty dollar bills.

"Uncle Jake sends his regards," I reply with a sly grin, as he laughs and shakes his head. Jori leans down and kisses me on the cheek before he asks the clerk where the restroom is, and then disappears to the back of the store.

I walk down the small aisles and grab some family sized bags of chips, and a couple of beef jerky sticks too, 'cause I know he loves them, and then head to the cooler and pick out a bottle of soda for each of us before I make my way back to the counter.

As the clerk begins to ring up my order, I clear my throat and glance around the store patiently.

"Oh, sir? Can I ask you a question?" I say, suddenly remembering I wanted to make sure we were headed in the right direction.

"You sure can, young lady," he replies with a nod as he finishes ringing up the items. I bite my lip and glance at the register, then hand him one of the twenty dollar bills to pay for everything.

"Which way is Canada? Like, are you on the

way there? Your station, I mean?" I inquire as I take my change from him and carefully fold up the loose bills before dropping the coins into a small donation box.

"You kids heading on a vacation or something?" he asks me curiously. I can already tell what he's thinking; that I look too young to hang out with Jori, but he's only three years older than me and I just happen to look really young for my age.

"Yeah," I reply with a big smile, picking up the bag from the counter. "So, um, are you?"

"You about ready?"

Jori reappears and wraps his arms tightly around my shoulders and resting his chin on the top of my head.

The clerk looks up at Jori, then smiles at me kindly. "You're just fine," he says in a low tone, before he turns his back to us and starts to fiddle with a carton of cigarettes.

"Thank you," I say quietly to his back as I let Jori lead me out of the store. I settle back into the passenger seat of the car as he begins to fuel it. Just like the man inside said, he has to go back in for his change, and as I watch him walk make his way back with his hands in his pockets, I let out a sigh.

We're traveling a road we don't even know, and

somehow, he's still managed to take me exactly where he wants to. Jori's always been able to do that somehow—go exactly wherever he's wanted without being worried about losing his way.

Maybe one day, I'll be like that too.

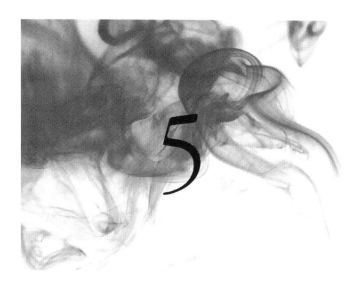

The Anvil, Present Day

Jori's tapping his fingers lightly on the tabletop as he watches me expectantly. My stomach turns under the weight of his eyes, and I push my half eaten plate of chips and salsa away.

"I have to go back," I say quietly as I lean my head down into my hand. "We didn't really do anything but just stare at each other for most of the visit."

It probably seems as lame as it sounds, but it's the truth. I said hello, he said hello, and then we spent the rest of the hour just looking at each other. Neither of us spoke for the most part, and to be honest, it was still one of the nicest visits I've ever had with someone.

I won't tell Jori that, though. I don't want him to think that any of the moments we've spent together aren't equal to the quiet hour I had with Hoyt.

Jori lets out a sigh, then cranes his neck, looking for Elizabeth. He waves her over, asks for another beer, and reaches into his pocket and tosses the car keys onto the table. I take them without a word and let drop them onto the empty space next to me.

Elizabeth returns with his beer and asks me if I'd like anything else.

"Coffee, please."

She nods and leaves the table.

"So, what exactly was the point of you going up there if you didn't have anything to say to him?" Jori asks tightly.

I cut my eyes toward Elizabeth, who's placing my cup down, a stirrer, and some packs of sugar. I'm hoping he'll be able to wait until she's gone again, and when he sips his beer, I'm relieved to know that he's heeding my silent request.

When she's out of earshot, I put my elbows on the table and look at him. "I didn't exactly plan on driving eight hours to not say anything to him. It *was* kind of a shock to see him after so long, you know."

Jori lets out a long breath and reaches across the table to take one of my hands in his. He runs his thumb over the top of my skin in an attempt to let me know that he's not as angry as he seems.

"I'm sorry, Red. I just don't want to go more days without being near you, you know? It sucked massively when you were gone, and I don't want to feel like that again. That's all," he explains gently.

I let out a sigh and look into his eyes. They're becoming glassy and unfocused. It's obvious that his intention is to drink himself deaf and dumb to my going back to see Hoyt, so he can claim that he didn't know I was going again.

"You can always come with me," I say slowly. "You won't be able to get into the actual prison, but we can rent a motel for a few days while I'm visiting with him."

Jori scoffs and lets go of my hand. It's still not good enough, but what else can I offer him? I'm not lying when I tell him that he can't get into Sing Sing. Hoyt would have to approve him for the visit, and he would have to fill out paperwork then wait to be approved by the warden, like I did, and considering he's not family, he would more than likely get denied.

"I can ask him when I see him. If he'll get you some papers, I mean," I say in a last ditch effort to quell the flames before they become far too intense for either of us to stew in any longer.

"Yeah, alright," he agrees indifferently. "You about ready to go?"

Before I have a chance to even taste my coffee, he chugs the rest of his beer, gets up from the table, and makes his way to the front of the restaurant. I roll my eyes and slide out of the booth. He'll calm down eventually, and when he does, maybe then I can tell him a little bit about what Hoyt looks like these days. He always looked up to him for some reason, though he never quite told me what it was.

Who knows? Maybe with the beer flowing through his veins, he may just open up and tell me.

As I walk toward the front of the restaurant where Elizabeth is ringing up our order, I try not to say anything further to upset him. Instead, I wrap my arms around his waist and lean my head against his back. He lets out a breath and turns his head slightly to glance down at me, a smile playing at the corner of his lips, and I close my eyes, savoring the semi-happy moment.

"Let's go," he says, as he slides his wallet back into his pocket and turns to wrap an arm around my shoulders.

"Thank you," I call out to her as we walk through the restaurant doors back into the night air.

Jori walks around the car to open the driver's side door for me, and as soon as I'm inside, he leans in and takes my face in his hands.

"I'm not angry at you, okay? I don't want you to think that, Red. I'm just in a really shitty mood because I've had to deal with Millie for the past few days, and then you tell me you're leaving again and I won't be able to stand that fucking cow so damn soon again." He crouches down and puts a hand on my leg. "I would very much like to go with you when you leave again, if that offer is still on the table."

I close my eyes for a moment and smile as the warmth of his hand on my leg keeps it safe from the cool breeze lazily wafting past us.

"It is, and I can't wait; it'll be like old times," I reply with a mischievous twinkle in my eye. He lets out a laugh before he leans in and kisses me softly on the lips. "Get in, Mr. Davidson; we've got some packing and prepping to do."

He walks quickly around the car and climbs into the passenger seat, pulls his seat-belt across his body, and holds out a hand palm up. As soon as I get the car going, I reach over and grasp it, letting our fingers interlace for the rest of the drive back.

We get home about twenty minutes later and walk into our dark, empty abode, laughing and happy for the moment because even though the road ahead of us won't be easy, we have each other to get through it, and that's what matters.

He rests his body weight against me as I attempt to lock the door, and giggles when I try to shrug him off.

"Not this time, kid," he whispers into my ear, grazing his lips against my neck. A shock goes through my body as I push back against him.

"Not anytime soon if you don't let me lock this damn place up," I reply with a shrill laugh.

Jori lets go of me, holding his hands up in the air, before clasping them behind his back and waiting patiently for me to make sure the lock is secured. I flip the deadbolt and turn the knob a few times to make sure we're safe for the night before I turn around and smile at him.

He's looking at me with heat and hunger in his eyes as he rubs his hands together and takes a step toward me. "You've got about a minute and a half before I have you bent over that fucking bed, so I would go say any prayers you feel like saying while I go get cleaned up," he says, biting his lower lip seductively.

I suddenly feel shy, and I'm not exactly sure why. This isn't the first time he's looked at me like that, nor is it the first time he's promised me a sound fucking, but maybe it's because I feel like I shouldn't be doing this so soon after seeing Hoyt.

I try to shrug it off as I walk quickly to the bedroom. I wish I had more time to tell him about seeing my father without him getting angry, but I guess I'll have plenty of time for that when we start the trip back up in a few days.

Once I get into the room, I pull my shirt over my head and toss it onto the floor, followed by my jeans—Jori will have to work for the rest.

I decide not to bend down and pray like he suggested, because God doesn't listen to me anymore. I know that, and it's okay, because some sinners who kneel and beg for mercy aren't worth redemption, and I'm one of them. If what I've suffered in my life isn't enough to have a blind eye turned to, then having Jori beside me would definitely suffice.

I push my hair behind my ears and climb onto the bed, pulling the sheet up to my neck and wait. I can hear Jori in the bathroom, humming drunkenly to himself, and I know the rest of the night will be fun.

I close my eyes and run my hands back through my hair. I let out a sigh when I notice Jori's humming has ceased, and try to relax as much as I can. I don't want him to think that I don't want to be with him, I just still haven't been able to shake Hoyt's eyes peering into me the way they did, and the last thing I want to envision when we're together is my father's face.

The door to the bedroom opens, then swings closed. I haven't peeked through my eyes yet, but smile when Jori climbs onto the bed and lowers himself gently onto my body.

"Hi," he says softly.

I finally open my eyes again and look at him.

"Hi," I reply, tilting my head.

His eyes are still glassy, but they're as serious as the look on his face. He leans down the rest of the way into me and runs a hand back over my head.

"Are you okay, Red?" he asks, using his hands to bring mine above my head. I nod slightly and a smile creeps across his handsome face. "Liar."

Jori's lips find their way to my neck and I shift slightly underneath him. He's always known how to kiss me gently enough to bring every nerve in my body to life, and the fact that he's not letting me touch him right now only adds fuel to the fire of my needing him.

"Feel that?" he breathes as he continues to lightly kiss my neck. *How can I miss it?* I nod and try to wriggle free of his grip, but he's put most of his strength into holding my wrists in place.

The kisses stop as quickly as they started, and he lifts his body, hovering over me with a curious look on his face.

"Would you be pissed if I put this off?" he asks.

I blink rapidly. Not once in the entire time we've been together has Jori even comprehended the words "put this off."

He lets out a laugh as he lets go of my wrists and drops his body onto the bed next to me. "I can tell you're not exactly here, you know? And I don't want to do this while you're still mentally in

Ossining. Besides, if you've got Hoyt on the brain while I'm fucking you, that'll bring back some shitty memories I don't want to be responsible for."

He's right about one thing; having Hoyt on the brain while Jori's inside me won't do good for either of us.

"Okay," I agree quietly.

He turns on his side, slides an arm around my waist, and lets out a sigh.

I didn't realize how grateful I would be for him backing off until I let out a yawn and turn my head toward him. I blink tiredly a few times and smile when I notice he's already passed out.

My sinner is sound asleep, and I know I won't be too far behind him.

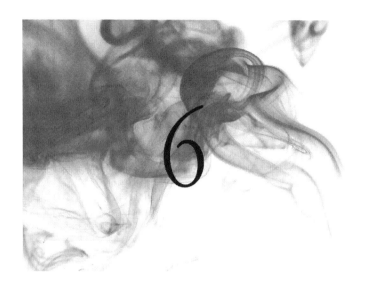

Binghamton, NY 1994

Jori says we should be halfway there, and we've decided to stop and stretch our legs for a bit. The air is much cooler in this part of New York, and it makes me shiver slightly.

"You okay, Red?" he asks, glancing down at me.

"Yeah," I reply with an enthusiastic nod. He laughs and squeezes my hand as we walk toward an intersection.

He left the car in a parking garage a few blocks back after I told him I found the town pretty.

That's when he got the idea to stretch our legs, but I know he's only doing it so I can explore and see new things. We settle on going to the zoo after seeing a few signs for it, partly because I love animals, and partly because it's the only thing we can really afford to do.

"This place looks kind of old," he remarks as we near the entrance. "But I bet it'll be a lot of fun."

I look up at him and grin. Even if the zoo doesn't live up to whatever expectations he thinks I have of it, I'm with him in a place neither of us has been to before, and that's more than enough for me.

"Two please," he says to the woman inside the booth. She tells him the admission for both of us is eight dollars, to which he reaches for his wallet and begins to carefully pull out one dollar bills like he did at the gas station.

It's not a quirk of his or anything, he's just always been very conscious about how much money he has on him and the amount he chooses to spend … Something about always making sure he has enough for bus fare if he ever needs it. While Jori continues his painfully slow count of the admission fee, as well as how much he has left, I reach into my bra again and slide a twenty dollar bill into the booth. He turns slightly and grunts at me. Obviously, he's upset that I'm paying for this, but if we stand around and wait for his meticulous money counting, the zoo will shut down and we won't have anything left to do.

"I could have paid for it, you know," he grumbles after we take the tickets and walk toward one of the staffers at the gate.

"I know. I just wanted to go in sometime today," I reply, making a face at him.

"Smart ass," he says with a laugh. I stick my tongue out at him and thank the young man who's smiling at our interaction as we walk into the zoo. Jori drapes an arm around my shoulder protectively, giving the man a pointed stare, before he begins to pull me off toward the carousel.

"Come on, Red! I'll race ya," he says with a grin as he pulls open the gate and waits for the carousel to come to a stop. I giggle as I run in behind him, wrapping my arms around him, as the machine comes to a complete halt. Jori takes me by the hand and walks us toward a couple of horses that are side by side, helping me up onto mine before he climbs onto his.

"Alright, I would hold on if I were you. I bet these things are fast," he instructs, rolling his eyes.

The "race" doesn't last more than a minute and a half, but we're both in great spirits when we walk away from the carousel. We spend no more than an hour and a half in the zoo, making sure to stop at each exhibit.

"I wish we had a camera. You look so happy here, Red. It would have been nice to capture that, you know?" Jori says, running his hand back through his hair as we make our way toward the gift shop.

"Memories make better pictures than film ever can," I reply happily with a twinkle in my eye. He smiles gratefully at me as he opens the door to the shop and waits for me to walk in first.

My eyes become huge and my heart flutters at all the stuffed animals inside. I pick up a meerkat and hold it up, smiling and giving it quick hug before I place it back down. That was definitely my favorite exhibit of the day, and if we had the time, I would have gone back in to see them again. While I would love to get a souvenir, I know they're far too expensive, and we'll have to find our way home at some point. We'll need every dime we have for that.

I give one last glance around the shop before making my way toward the exit, waving at the two teenage girls behind the registers. They smile and wave back at me, which makes me feel good about things. Usually, strangers don't care too much for me and Jori being around, but they seemed genuine with their smiles.

"I guess we should head back to the car now," I say, turning to look at Jori. I raise my eyebrows and begin to wring my hands when I realize he's not there, and I crane my neck toward the zoo exit, wondering where he could be.

I sit down on the green, metal bench just outside the entrance, and wonder where he could have wandered off to.

Time ticks by slowly, and I know it hasn't been more than five minutes, but it worries me that I lost him in a place I don't know.

"Goddamn, you're fast," he calls out with a laugh as he appears a few moments later. I leap up from the bench and start walking quickly toward him, but he shakes his head and grins, "Close your eyes, Red."

"Why?" I ask him in confusion, stopping in my tracks.

"Because I said so. Close them," he replies chuckling.

"On the count of three, you can open them

again, okay?" he says. I nod and close my eyes tighter than ever before as he slowly begins to count. "One ... two ... two and a half ..."

"Jori!" I shout, gleefully.

"Sorry, I couldn't help myself," he replies with a chuckle. "Two and three quarters ..." I put my hands on my hips and let out a sigh, to which he snickers, and finally says three.

When I open my eyes again, my hands fly to my mouth in shock. He's holding out the meerkat I had held so happily for only a few moments, and he looks so proud of himself when my face lights up.

"Thank you!" I exclaim as I rush forward and take the stuffed animal from his hands. I hug it tightly again and look up into his eyes. His face is red, and as he slides his hands into his pockets, I can feel something is different about him. What it is, I can't quite place yet, but it's enough to make me feel incredibly shy for some reason.

"I know we can't afford this," I say softly. "But I promise you this will be my most prized possession for the rest of my life, and I'll pay you back somehow. I promise."

"Um, you don't have to pay me back," he says, looking down at his feet and kicking the ground. "I just wanted you to have it because I saw how happy it made you."

I take a step closer to him and wrap my free arm around his body, leaning my head against his chest, and he chuckles. He pulls his hands out of his pockets and returns my hug, his heartbeat increasing from somewhere deep inside his chest.

"We should probably go back to the car," he says softly.

I nod and begin to pull away, but as I do, he leans his face down and kisses me gently on the lips. It takes us both by surprise, because up until now, we've only ever been best friends. True, we have a song and he calls me babe from time to time, but it's never meant anything other than what we've actually said to each other.

"I'm sorry," he says, pulling away, wide-eyed and embarrassed.

"I ... I've never had a boy kiss me before," I reply shakily, hugging my meerkat tightly. Jori runs his hands back through his hair and looks away. He looks as shocked as we both feel, and it bothers me. Maybe he can be more than a friend, but is it really worth messing up our perfect friendship to find out?

"Maybe we can do that again sometime?" I ask, tripping over my words as I try to catch his eyes.

He turns his face back toward me and grins, looking faint with relief. "Anytime you want, Red."

I smile shyly as he puts his arm around my waist and we begin to walk. "We should probably get going toward Canada again. I got something really cool there I want to show you."

I let him lead me back to the car, completely disregarding the fact that he's just told me a secret. I don't care that he's been there without me already; I just care that we're going there together.

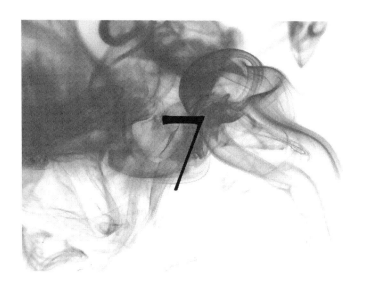

Present Day

I awake with a start.

My body is covered in sweat and my heart is racing much too fast for only having been asleep. I turn slightly to glance at Jori, pushing my damp hair out of my face. Somehow, he managed to sleep through my rocking the bed as violently as I did. His mouth is slightly open and his quiet snoring helps fill the otherwise silent room.

I ease myself off the side of the bed and walk as quietly as I can to the bathroom. Once inside, I close the door and sit on the edge of the bathtub. I had the dream again, and if I tell him that, he'll encourage me to brush it off like he always does.

Jori doesn't like talking about that particular dream that usually only comes back to haunt me when something ominous is on the horizon.

He doesn't care much for the past because he says it's behind us for a reason, and that's where it should stay. I beg to differ, but we've had that argument one too many times and it's the only time I ever see him angry these days.

I take a few deep breaths before I get back to my feet and push the shower curtain aside. Maybe if I spend some time in a hot cascade of water, I can ignore the fact that things are trying to come back to haunt me when they should be dead and buried.

Once I have the temperature slightly above what I'm comfortable with, I pull my panties and bra off, tossing them into the hamper. I walk over to the small linen closet we keep our towels in and grab one, tossing it over the top of the curtain rod and step in.

I let my breath out in a rush. As it turns out, the water is a little more than slightly above my level of comfort, but I'll take the punishment for the secrets I've kept, and for the ones that are trying to find their way into the light again.

I reach for my shower gel, then my loofah, squeezing a generous amount onto it, before I begin to scrub myself.

Dirty little girls are the devil's handiwork. I've heard that about as often as being told I was hated, but the two always went hand in hand, and I never cared enough to try and discern them.

I lived with constantly being told I was dirty, and I hid whenever I heard the whispers of sweet candy, and all the while I had lost myself in trying to be the perfect daughter. I never got to know the true Gracie until Jori started spiriting me away to his tree house on my loneliest nights.

The more I think about it, the more I'm surprised that Millie never caught us up there; Uncle Jake knew about it—he told me as much, but he also reasoned that we were just kids, and that if he couldn't make me feel better about everything that happened, at least someone could.

I let out a grunt and open my eyes; I've scratched myself with my nails and there are small trails of blood starting to run down my arm. I have to be much more careful with cleaning myself up, because if Jori sees the small nicks and cuts, he'll know.

I let the loofah fall to the shower floor and decide to shampoo my hair. No matter how hard I've tried, I've never really been able to pull that out completely, and since it's so damn thick and red, he won't see if I hurt myself that way.

Penance, I correct myself. It's such a bullshit thought; neither Momma nor Daddy were religious, and I was put through hell for sins I never committed. Maybe that's why when things went south and I got a better understanding of how the world worked, I went ahead and racked up a few of my own.

"Good morning," comes the sleepy voice as the door to the bathroom swings open.

I jump at the sound of Jori entering the room, but I manage to mumble a good morning as cheerfully as I can muster, and let out a sigh when I hear the toilet lid being lifted. I step as far under the water as I can so I don't have to listen to him relieve himself while I'm trying to shower.

I can tell that today will be one of *those* days. Everything is going to bother me and he'll think he's done something wrong, and no matter how much I tell him it's not him, he won't believe me.

I turn around and lean my head back into the downpour as I wash the shampoo out of my hair. My eyes are closed tightly as I purposely grab two handfuls of hair and pull them as hard as I can, but I stop almost immediately when I feel hands on my waist.

Jori pulls my slick body toward his and holds me tightly as I attempt to untangle my hands from my hair. He scoffs when he realizes what I was doing, and keeps an arm wrapped firmly around me, while he uses his other hand to help me free myself from the bondage of pain I've set on my head. He kisses each hand as it's pulled free, then takes each one and wraps them around his neck.

"Stop doing that to yourself," he says softly. "There's nothing bothering you that can't be talked about. I may not be able to fix all your problems, Red, but I can at least listen to them and let you blow off some steam."

I nod and lower my head. I don't want him to see my trembling lip, and I damn sure don't want him to mistake the anger in my tears for weakness.

"Red?" he says as he gently places his lips on my forehead.

I clear my throat and look back into his eyes, trying my best to smile, but instead a sob escapes me as I bury my head into his bare chest and begin to cry.

Jori runs his hands back over my hair and rocks me slowly back and forth. Simple things like this make all the difference in the world to me, and he knows it.

And that's why I can't ruin him with the secret I swore I would keep.

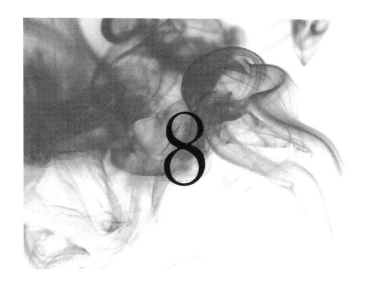

Sing Sing Correctional Facility, 1997

I think the use of so much white in this goddamn place is designed to make the inmates go crazy. Death Row is no better—twenty-three fucking hours on lockdown for the "bad" guys here, and maybe, if you're lucky, an hour of rec time somewhere that isn't white.

I learned that lesson the hard way, but when you're a big guy, the new kids here try to fight you to prove they're worth the balls hanging from their body. I've smashed enough heads in my day that I don't need to fight anyone else to prove my worth, but these little fuckers—they just keep coming for me.

The Warden gets it these days, though. He's told me that any time I spend in AD-SEG isn't because of defending myself, it's to keep the other inmates safe from me.

"Blackburn! You've got mail!"

I raise an eyebrow and lift my head off my cot slightly. Officer Davis is a good guy; he's always treated me with the same respect I treat the rest of the C.Os. I think in a way, he knows the truth, but he won't tell anyone because he's not entirely sure.

Hell, even I don't know what the fucking truth is anymore.

"From whom?" I ask, looking at him curiously.

He looks down at the small envelope in his hand and reads the return address to me.

"G. Blackburn," he recites, holding it through my cell bars.

The palms of my hands begin to sweat as I throw my legs over the side of the cot and get to my feet. It's not possible, is it? She couldn't have possibly written me a letter when I was so damn sure that everyone convinced her I was the devil incarnate.

"You alright? You look shaky all of a sudden," Davis remarks as he raises an eyebrow at me.

"Yeah, man. I'm fine. Thanks," I say with a nod, as I take the letter from him and go back to my prison-issued bed. It's the most uncomfortable thing I've ever slept on, and some nights I prefer the floor to the itchy blanket and impossibly flat mattress.

I wait until Davis makes his way to the next cell before I turn the letter over and look at the return address. I have to see it with my own eyes for it to be true, but there it is—plain as fucking day. *G. Blackburn.*

I let out a shaky breath as I flip the envelope over again and tear the back off. I've spent a lot of sleepless nights on the floor, wondering if my baby girl hated me, and I have a feeling that this letter will hold the answer.

The paper is neatly folded equally in three, and I can almost swear I smell her on it. I look up at the ceiling as I carefully open it before I decide to rip off the proverbial band-aid and look down to read.

The handwriting is different from what I remember, but she's grown up a lot since then, so that's to be expected. It's the first line—the salutation—that renders me to tears as I do my best to read what she's written to me without bawling like a baby.

Dear Daddy,

I want you to know that I miss you. I love you lots and I don't believe what they're saying about you.

Would it be possible to visit you sometime?

I hope so.

Love,

Gracie.

It's one of the shortest letters I've ever read, yet it holds the most meaning of anything the world can ever offer me. Reassurance from my own flesh and blood that she still loves me; that she's not afraid of me, and believes me to be a good man.

I wipe the tears from my face and let out a soft laugh. Gracie has always been the one good thing in my life—the constant reminder that while I may never have been the best father or husband in the fucking world, just once, I had gotten something right.

"My special girl," I say softly, with a shake of my head as I fold the letter back up and slip it into the envelope. I lean back and slide the letter under my pillow and lie back down.

We named her after my mother; partly because she looks so damn much like her, and partly because it was another way to stick it to Doreen. Of course, had I known the kind of mother that bitch would have been, I would've taken Gracie and run far away from Cold Spring.

It was so fucking hard to keep my baby girl safe from that psychopath, working the long hours I did, but I would take her to work with me the days Doreen had drugged herself into a stupor. It was against company policy to have such a little girl in the scrapyard, but she wore her hard hat "just like Daddy", as she would proudly say, and she always watched from the office window while I worked.

I never knew just how bad shit had gotten, because Doreen wouldn't bruise Gracie where I could see. Usually, she'd come to me crying if I came home late from work, and when I would try to hug her and ask her what was wrong, she would let out a squeal of pain.

That's how I knew she was abusing her. I didn't have any solid proof, because every time I attempted to check my baby's body for any marks, she would scream at me that I was being inappropriate with Gracie, and how she would call the cops and have me arrested for touching my baby.

I never did, though. I *never* fucking put a hand on my little girl; in anger or any other way.

The last day I was at work before it happened, Gracie looked up at me with her big brown eyes and told me I was her hero.

Something snapped in me after that. If I was her hero, how come I couldn't save her? Isn't that what a hero does? Save those that can't save themselves?

I cross my arms behind my head and stare up at the white ceiling in this sickly white room, and wonder about the little white lies that had been fed to her after I got arrested.

I've never been able to prove my word to anyone in halls of the judicial system, and when the court sees fit, they'll set a date for me to get a needle to the arm, signed off by the governor himself.

I close my eyes and sigh. I'll ask Davis for some paper and a pen when he comes back. I'll get some stamps from the commissary with the little bit of cash I have in there, and I'll write Gracie back. I'll tell her that prison is no place for her to be, and that even though I love her and miss her so fucking much, it's better if she remembers the good times we had and not have to walk down these halls.

These halls are for killers, thieves, rapists ... the scum of the fucking Earth. My baby girl doesn't belong here.

Neither do I, I think as I turn on my side and stare at the white wall that silently stares back at me.

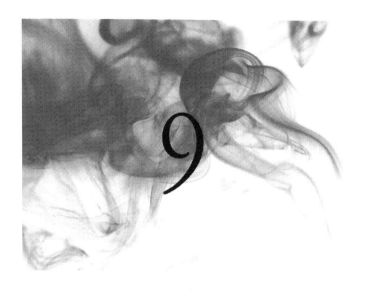

Present Day

"Hey, so did I show you what I got while you were gone?" Jori asks, settling next to me on the couch.

After I had my little meltdown in the shower, he held me until our skin wrinkled and I calmed down, and then dried us both off. Sometimes, I think the weight of my conscience will drive him away, but he doesn't seem to scare easy. If he did, he would have left me a long time ago.

"No," I reply, smiling as much as I can at his obvious enthusiasm.

"You're gonna love this; it's so cool. Wait here and close your eyes," he says like the excited boy who once drove me so far away from home.

I lean back against the couch, cross my arms loosely over my chest, and close my eyes like he asked me to. I can hear his footsteps moving quickly toward the back of our home, and then return not a few moments later. I don't mind that it's not a big place, because it's home, and it's enough for just the two of us.

Jori lets out an excited laugh as he sits back down next to me. His knee brushes my leg when he brings his up on the couch, and I'm hoping he's not still wearing his house shoes. I'm not a germaphobe by any means, but I've just spent the last thirty minutes crying in a shower because I didn't feel like I was clean enough, and this would be enough for a repeat performance from me.

"Keep your eyes closed while I tell you this," he says as he leans the side of his body against the couch. "So okay, while I was at Millie's listening to her moo and bitch at me for showing up unannounced, I went down into the rec room and looked around for a bit. The bitch knew better than to follow me down there 'cause it's soundproof, remember? Anyway, that's not the point. I couldn't sleep, so I started looking through the boxes and shit, and I found this and couldn't believe that I forgot it was even there—I actually kind of felt like a piece of shit when I saw it, but it's okay now, 'cause I have it and … well. Open your eyes, Red," he finishes in a rush.

"I'm not sure I want to," I reply with a nervous giggle.

"Oh come on! You're gonna love this!" he exclaims happily.

I take a deep breath and purse my lips. What Jori could have possibly found in the basement of Millie's place that's making him so excited right now is beyond me, but I don't want to disappoint him—I'm sure I've done that enough in the past few days.

I open one eye slowly, then the other, and turn to face him. I gasp as my hand flies to my mouth and the smile on his face widens into a huge grin covering most of his face.

"Wow," I say softly as I reach over and take the vinyl record from his hands. It's Stone Temple Pilots—the Thank You album—and it's old and dusty, yet somehow shiny and brand new.

"Look," he says, leaning over and flipping the record over. Jori leans his head against mine as his finger grazes down the song list on the back until it stops just where I knew it would. "It's our song."

I let out a sigh as I place my hand on his and smile up at him. "Remember that time we drove to Canada?"

"Oh God," he replies, rolling his eyes with a laugh. "That was a fucking disaster."

"That's not how I remember it," I reply, looking back down at the record. Next to the meerkat he got me on that trip, this may be my favorite possession in the world, and I want to tell him that, but I'm sure he knows it.

"Let's talk about Hoyt," I suggest, changing the subject.

Jori's body goes slightly rigid against me, and he sighs heavily. I know he was hoping I wouldn't bring this up again, but I didn't want to keep talking about my plans to go back yet, because he started downing beers as soon as I mentioned it.

"We have to—the trip is in a couple of days, and we need to get our accommodation taken care of at the very least," I say, placing the record on the coffee table and getting to my feet. I glance around the living room for my laptop and spot it on the love seat. I walk over and retrieve it, settling back down on the couch next to Jori, who's gone from happy to agitated in the small amount of time it took me to bring up the trip back to Ossining.

He runs a hand irritably over his face, which I choose to ignore, as I power the laptop on. Once the lock screen shows up, I lean forward and type in my password and wait for the background to populate. Jori knows the password to the laptop too, because we made it up one night together; however, we both have things on there that would get us in a shit ton of trouble if the machine got into the wrong hands.

"Red?" he asks, as I lean back and watch the screen.

"Hm?" I reply absentmindedly.

"Kiss me."

"In a minute," I say as the background picture begins to populate. I don't want to get too lost in a moment right now that I forget to look for a cheap hotel room for us to reserve.

"No," he says softly, as he pulls me back against him, and brushes my hair out of my face. "Now."

Jori presses his lips gently against mine, and my breath catches in my throat. His hands find their way to my hips and he pulls me onto his lap. I won't deny him any longer—he's been patient enough.

I decide to lose myself in his kiss, our tongues swirling together as he reaches his hands up the back of my shirt and unclips my bra. I pull back with a smile, and Jori lets out a breathy chuckle as he pulls my shirt off my body and I shrug the undergarment off.

He leans back for a moment and looks at my perky tits, his eyes becoming hazy with lust and desire, before he grabs one and gently begins to suck and nibble on my nipple. I close my eyes and arch my back—the feel of his tongue on my bare skin has always been intoxicating, and this is no different. He moves his mouth from my left breast to the right, hungrily suckling my nipple before biting down a little harder than usual, causing me to yelp.

"Watch it," I reply, playfully giving him a gentle shove.

"Fuck that," he growls. Grabbing me by the hips again, he lowers me onto the couch and begins to pull my shorts off, kissing my inner thighs as he does.

I'm mad with need for him as he throws them to the floor, then positions himself between my legs. Gently, he begins to rub my clit over my panties, and I can feel the warmth beginning to pool against the soft fabric.

"Just like fresh hyacinth on a warm spring day," he murmurs, as he slides my panties aside and inhales deeply.

He uses the tip of his tongue to gently tease my clit, and I reach down, grabbing a handful of his hair. Jori smiles against my pussy as he brings a finger up and starts to run it up and down my slit. The sensation is something I can't quite describe, but this man has always known my body better than anyone else, and he uses that knowledge to keep me satisfied.

"Nah," he suddenly says, pulling away from my exposed pussy. "I'd rather open you back up with my dick."

A wicked grin spreads across his handsome face as he gets up, pulls his pants off, hovering for just a moment so I can see how hard his cock is, before he yanks off his boxers and tosses them onto the pile of clothes we've made on the floor. Jori then moves back to hover over me, but I bring my legs together tightly and shake my head.

"My turn," I say, pulling at his shirt. He yanks it over his head and laughs, then sits back on the couch, watching me with those bitter blue eyes.

"If you insist," he replies with a smirk.

I prop myself up on my knees as best I can before I wet my palm with my tongue and reached for his cock. I run my hand up and down his length, which makes him lean his head back against the arm of the couch and take in sharp breaths. I can't help but smile, because this man could have any woman in the world he wants, yet he's always so eager to have *me.*

"Come on, Red," he half-whines, half-pleads. A smirk creases my face, but I comply as I lean down and take the head of his cock into my mouth.

Jori gently places a hand on the back of my head, careful not to push down before I'm ready. I work my mouth down his length, slowly, deliberately, savoring the taste of him as I reach a hand down and grip his balls. He always loves that—a mouth on his dick and a hand working his balls at the same time. It's the fastest way to get him off, but I want to be able to indulge him in this moment, so I stop after a few minutes and move my body on top of his.

"What the fuck?" he breathes with a chuckle. "Why did you stop?"

"Because," I reply with a shrug.

"Well, that's not fair," he says, folding an arm

behind his head. I smile at him, which he returns, and raise an eyebrow. If he thinks this was the most of what was going to happen right now when I'm wet with desire for him, I guess I should prove him wrong.

I bite my lower lip and reach down for his still hard cock, and lower myself onto it. It's been a while since Jori and I last fucked, which makes for a better time, I like to think.

My pussy is tighter, and his cock will realize this once it's inside me, which will make him even harder and more animalistic. Jori grips my hips tightly and begins to gently push up as I continue to slowly lower myself onto his cock, before he's finally inside.

"Oh *fuck*. I have missed this so much," he says, in a thick voice as I reach down and grab his wrists. I slowly begin to move back and forth, until I've found a pace we're both comfortable with. He moves his hands up to my sides, fingers digging in so deeply, I could almost swear he's trying to crush me.

I use his force—his overwhelming need of me —arch my back, and begin to grind my hips into him. Jori lets out a loud moan, then begins to thrust up into me. I gasp and move my hands from his wrists to his forearms, trying my best not to fold against him and let him fuck me, but it's no use. My body attempts to collapse against him, but he stops me, holding me at bay with a hand around my throat.

"Uh uh," he breathes through gritted teeth. "You need to keep those tits bouncing. I wanna see your face when you come for me."

His hand tightens around my neck as he slowly begins to deprive me of air, fucking me harder than he ever has before, and I attempt to pry his hand loose. He slaps my tits as he thrusts faster into me, and I moan as loudly as I can through the air deprivation. It only makes him squeeze my neck harder, fuck me faster, and make me come so fucking hard I damn near pass out. I feel the warmth of his cum rush into me as he groans and falls back against the couch.

"Goddamn, I love you," he whispers, pulling me against him and holding me close. My body is trembling, my legs feel like jello, and my throat is raw, but Jori is happy, and that's all that matters to me.

We're both coated in sweat from our quick, brutal morning fuck, and I can smell the scent of our efforts beginning to fill the living room. I chuckle and place my hands on his chest, pushing myself up slightly to look at him. He tilts his head and grins at me expectantly.

"Jori Davidson, did you just try to kill me?" I ask him in mock surprise.

"Nah; just your pussy," he replies, wiggling his eyebrows. "And the way I felt it hugging my dick, I'm pretty sure I did my job."

"Always so modest," I say, playfully rolling my eyes. I lie my head back down against his chest. There will be time to worry about a hotel room later. For now, I just want to savor the moment of being in the arms of the man whose love is as dangerous as the look in his eyes, and as brutal as the intentions hidden behind his mischievous grin.

He makes me feel needed, wanted, and loved; things I had lost when Hoyt was taken from me, and I refuse to lose Jori, too. And while I may have my fair share of secrets, I know Jori has some too.

10

Buffalo, NY 1994

"Is that Niagara Falls?" I ask Jori excitedly, gripping his arm. I can see the huge wonder looming in the distance, and I can't stop the young girl who's so amazed by the sight coming to the surface.

"Yep," he replies with a grin. He checks the side-view mirror, then exits the highway, driving another thirty minutes down the road until he can pull over.

"Come on," he says, getting out of the car.

Before I have a chance to push my door open, he's by my side of the car, pulling it open for me and making a grand, sweeping gesture with his arm. I giggle and step out, holding my meerkat stuffed animal to my chest, and taking his hand with the other.

Jori leads the way toward a massive bridge that sits directly in front of the Falls, and we stop to read the plaque at the entrance.

"I thought the Rainbow Bridge was for dead pets?" I ask him in confusion.

"That's a different one, Red. Come on, let's take a walk over to Canada, shall we?" he says, reaching into his pocket with his free hand. We head toward the fare collector and pay the seventy-five cents a piece to cross. The collector advises us that we can walk *to* Canada, but can't enter without a passport because if they let us in, we wouldn't be able to cross back over.

We both nod, and Jori looks at me a little dejectedly, but I just shrug indifferently and it seems to perk him back up. It's nighttime now, and the bridge is lit up brightly, making the majesty of the Falls even grander than they would more than likely be in the daytime.

"I guess it depends on the person at the booth,"

he says to me with a sheepish grin. "I've walked across the border before and back again."

"When?" I ask him curiously, as we step onto the bridge and begin our little trek toward the Canadian border.

"Um, remember that time that I was gone for like, a week? After I got into it with Millie a couple of years ago? Well, I decided I couldn't take any more of her shit. She ended up slapping me and because I knew if I hit her back I wouldn't let up until I killed her miserable ass; I grabbed her keys and took off in the car," he explains with a shrug. Suddenly, Jori stops walking and looks down at me nervously. "I mean, I know I shouldn't be complaining about my home life to you, but I only do it 'cause you're the one person who listens to me, you know?"

I roll my eyes and smile. "I'm not some fragile kid, Jori. If I haven't broken yet over what happened, don't expect it to happen anytime soon. Besides, I like that you're able to talk to me and tell me things; it makes me feel special."

Jori's face softens as he pulls me to one side of the bridge and looks down into my eyes.

"You *are* special, Red. When are you gonna realize that?" he asks softly.

I shrug again and turn away from him. I'm close to tears, and I hate it. I hate that every time he tries to make me understand that I'm worth more than the "dirty girl" I was made to believe I was, it feels like a lie. He's my best friend, though, and I try my best to believe him, even when I feel like I can't.

Be strong, just like Daddy.

"Hey, so what did you do while you were across the border?" I ask, wiping away a stray tear and clearing my throat. I bring myself up on my tiptoes and lean over the railing to get a glimpse of the water below us.

Jori crosses his arms on the railing next to me and shifts uncomfortably. I glance over at him and knit my eyebrows expectantly, but he's too busy scuffing his sneakers against the stone walkway to notice.

"Jori?" I ask with a nervous laugh. "What did you do over there?"

A million and one thoughts are running through my mind, but only one scenario sticks out the most. I remember the one time we were in school and I saw him in the hallway talking to the most popular girl in the entire building—Ashley, I think her name was. They looked so cozy together,

THE LIES BETWEEN US

him leaning one hand against the locker and her holding her books to her chest, gingerly running a hand down the inside of his jacket, that it made me feel sick and sad at the same time.

I didn't speak to him for weeks after that, and I made it a point to avoid him as much as I could. Whenever he would come over, I would have Uncle Jake turn him away. It made him angry and depressed, and it took him sitting me down and explaining to me that the reason he looked so comfortable with her was because he wanted to be sure he had her attention.

Ashley was something of a mean girl when it came to me. She always had a snide remark or two about what Hoyt had done, that I was such a loser Uncle Jake was forced to take me instead of being given an option.

I hated her, and Jori knew it, but I could never shake how happy they looked that day, talking to each other, and I wouldn't put it past her to have sweet talked him into a trip to Canada to make it up to him for being so rotten with me.

"Ashley?" I ask him quietly.

"What?" he asks in complete horror. "What the fuck made you even think of that slag?"

I shrug and turn my body toward him. He sighs

deeply and sees in my eyes that I'm worried there was more to that little meeting than I was led to believe.

"You know the reason I got kicked out of school was because of that, right? She tried to put the moves on me after I blew her off, and she told the guidance counselor that I threatened her," he recounts with a shrug. "But she left you alone, so whatever."

Jori shudders as he looks up at the night sky. "God, Red. I can't believe you would actually think that."

"Sorry," I reply softly.

He shrugs again and turns his eyes toward me. "Alright. I have to tell you something, but you have to promise that you won't ask me any questions and you won't be pissed at me. I'll tell you more about it when you're older, but things are still fresh, and I don't want to open those wounds back up again so soon, okay?"

"Okay," I reply curiously.

He takes in a deep breath and lets it out in a rush. I watch Jori as he rubs the back of his neck and glances up and down the bridge to make sure no one is in earshot before he begins to talk.

"I ... um." He clears his throat and scuffs his

sneakers against the stone again, stealing a glance at me. "I was there when it happened. I mean, I saw what happened—it was a total accident. I heard the arguing when I was up in my tree house, and I wanted to make sure that you were okay, you know? Uh ... you weren't there, though. Hoyt told me he had sent you to Jake's that night before Doreen got home, and that he needed my help hiding some shit. I took a box from him and ran back home because I didn't want to see Doreen's body. I don't think I'd ever be able to shake something like that from my mind. Anyway," he says, coughing one time, "I took that box and snuck back into my little man cave and stuck that shit into a hole in the wall and bricked it up. I had actually forgotten about it for a few years until you started bringing him up again, and that's when I went back to get it and came up here."

My mouth is dry. I feel like I've been chewing on a mouthful of cotton, and that the only person in the world who still gives a shit about me is nothing more than someone else who's been stuck with me instead of actually wanting me around.

I take a ragged breath, turn around, and toss the meerkat over the railing. The look of confusion on Jori's face is mixed with shock and a bit of pain as I turn from him and run back across the bridge.

"Red! GRACIE!" he yells out, as he attempts to catch up to me.

I don't know where I'm going, and I don't know how far my legs will take me, but I refuse to be the used, dirty little girl who's a burden and unworthy of being truly wanted.

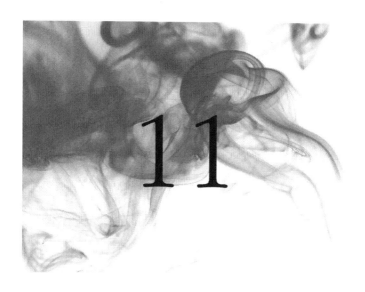

Last Weekend

I've spent years trying to convince Gracie not to come up here, but she's stubborn just like me, and today is visiting day. I've never been as nervous in my entire life as I was when I woke up this morning, and one would think I'd be getting led to the fucking gurney, not to see my kid.

Davis brought me a new comb and told me he'd take me to the showers so I could shave and get cleaned up before she gets here. Normally, C.Os won't escort an inmate on something as mundane as that, but he has kids too, so he gets it.

"You about ready, Blackburn?"

I stop pacing my cell and glance at the bars. Davis is there with a towel and his ring of keys in his hands. As soon as I nod, he unlocks my cell and pulls the door open.

"Come on then," he instructs with a nod. I fall into step beside him and am grateful he hasn't put cuffs on me. Death Row in Sing Sing has its own facilities apart from gen pop that the Warden lets me use, so I won't have to worry much about any of the new kids today trying to take me down for being the resident "big guy."

I'm in such good spirits by the time we get to the showers that I could go straight to the death house after this and die a happy man, having laid eyes on my baby one last time.

I turn the faucets and get a temperature I can handle, open a fresh bar of soap, and start washing myself up as best I can. I don't want to smell like just another fucking guy in the clink when I see her. I want to be presentable, and maybe look as much like the man she probably remembers.

As I turn my back to the wall and begin to soap up my hair, it suddenly hits me that Gracie isn't the little girl *I* remember. Hell, she's a grown woman now, and I wonder if she still looks like both me and Doreen, or if she looks like her own person these days.

I wonder if she's maybe a momma at this point; if she's married, or even hooked up with someone. I have a thousand and one questions I want to ask her, and in a couple of hours, I'll get to do just that.

I let out a breath as I finish washing the soap out of my hair, then go over my body one more time with the bar, making sure that at the very least, I'll smell like this generic bullshit, as opposed to sweat and regret. Gracie deserves much better than what I can give her, but I'm gonna do my best to not look or smell like a piece of shit when I see her.

I turn the water off and walk over to the partition, grabbing the towel and wrapping it securely around my waist. I walk over to the entrance and ask Davis for the comb before I make my way to the mirrors lined on the opposite wall of the showers and wipe away the steam with the palm of my hand.

"Goddamn," I say to myself, with a shake of my head. I didn't care much before about how I look these days, but now I have a reason to, there's not much I can do about it. I've been inside for fifteen fucking years, waiting for this nightmare to finally end, and I look like I'm heading toward sixty instead of fifty.

If I live to see fifty, that makes Gracie ... twenty-four?

I sigh when I realize just how much of her life I've missed. I pull the towel free from my waist and rub my hair, drying it as best I can, before I start to run the comb through it. I could do with a shave too, but Davis has done enough for me and I don't want him to get into any shit over my visit today.

After spending a few more moments staring at an old man I don't quite remember, I secure the towel back around my waist and walk to the entrance of the showers.

"I'm ready to go back to my cell, man," I say to him, sliding my feet into the standard issued prison slippers he brought for me.

"Where are your clothes?" he asks me, raising an eyebrow.

"Got a fresh shirt and pants on my cot. I didn't wanna get them wet. It's a quick walk, Davis. Please?" I ask, glancing down into his face.

He rubs his chin for a second, then nods, and we make our way back to my cell.

"I'll be back just before she gets here to come for you. Got some rules and shit we gotta go over before I take you up there," he says after I step into my cell and he locks the door.

I nod and wait for him to leave, before dropping the towel to the ground and pulling on a fresh pair of boxers. Even those are white—like the shirt, my pants, and the fucking walls that stare at me day in and day out. I refuse to be angry today, and I won't let the overwhelming bland color get to me; not when I know Gracie is on her way, if not already here.

She's always been like me—early for everything. *Ten minutes early is better than five minutes late, right Daddy?* I close my eyes and sigh as I pull my pants up and think of her tiny voice and how she would always repeat little things I said to her. Only the good stuff, though. Gracie never uttered a bad word that I would yell at Doreen, and I tried my best to shield her from that bullshit, but life has a weird way of bringing out the worst in people when you try your damnedest to be good.

I sit down on the edge of my cot after I'm dressed, and pull out the numerous letters she's sent to me over the years from beneath my pillow where I have them for safekeeping. I open each one, from the very first one she sent, and start to reread them while I wait for the time to go by.

Davis returns about an hour and a half later, as he promised, opens the cell door, and produces some shackles.

"Rule number one: you've gotta be chained up while we walk to the visiting room. I won't be going with you, but Officer Morgan here will," he says, nodding at the newest C.O. who's standing next to him, eyeing me warily.

I slide the letters back under my pillow, nod, and get to my feet. As they proceed to wrap the chain around my waist and connect it to cuffs at the wrists and ankles, I listen as Davis continues with his rules. Well, I'm not listening, really; I'm more interested in getting up to the room and seeing my kid, but I do a damn good job of acting like I'm paying attention—so much so that when Davis leaves me with Morgan, I decide the best thing to do is keep my mouth shut and let him lead me to where I need to go.

The new kid is nice—very talkative, even if I don't respond to him right away, and he seems genuine like Davis does, so after we get past the other cell blocks and up to the main floor, I open up and start joking with him.

Twenty-five minutes later, we're walking down a hallway I'm not familiar with, and my nerves begin to fray. I'm getting closer to Gracie than I have in fifteen fucking years, and the thought is turning my stomach in the best way possible.

In her letters, she always signs them *love Gracie,* and now I'll be able to look into her eyes and see if she really does still love me.

A few more steps, and Morgan puts his hand on my elbow, stopping me short. "I'll unchain you once we get inside. I hate to do that to you in front of your kid, but that's part of the rules."

I nod as he pulls the door open, and as he damn near trips and falls, I start laughing. He turns to look at me and chuckles, holding the door open to let me go in first. I don't look at Gracie right away because I'm afraid that I'll burst into fucking tears, and that's not the man she remembers.

Once we're inside the small room, I glance up at Davis, careful not to look at Gracie yet, and he nods at me as he begins to say some shit I can't hear through the glass. Morgan tells me to raise my arms to my waist, and he leans down to uncuff me. He wraps the chains around his arms and tells me he'll be right outside the door.

"You have one hour," he reminds me, giving me a pat on the shoulder.

I take a deep breath as I sit down and finally look at my Gracie—my one last thing worth fighting for. I reach for the phone and chuckle when I realize she's still very much like me, not looking up right away, but when she does … my God, when she does … I let my breath out in a rush and smile at her as she picks up her phone and says the sweetest words I've heard in a very long time.

"Hi, Daddy."

12

Present Day

Red's got her back to me as she starts to type on her laptop. I run a hand down her naked, sweaty spine, and smile when she shivers slightly, casting me a glance over her shoulder. I'm not too excited about going to see Hoyt, but I'd be even less excited about having to spend more time with Millie, so I'll let her drag me on this magical voyage back to New York and see what comes of it.

I fold an arm behind my head and snake the

other around her waist. She doesn't react because she's so into her fucking research, so I decide to let my hand make its way up her body until I've got a firm grip on her right breast. She sighs, but it doesn't deter me from grabbing her nipple and giving it a gentle tug.

The sound she makes—the quiet, sharp intake of her breath—is enough to start making me hard again.

"Not now, Jori. Please," she says, pulling my hand away, and I sigh heavily.

I get that we just fucked, but I can never get enough of her, and the fact that she's so wrapped up in something I'm completely against bugs the shit out of me. I won't tell her, though—I don't want to end up having her hate me because I think it's a terrible idea that she's trying to get close to Hoyt again. Especially since his number should be up any day now, but Red seems to have a thing for setting herself up for disappointment with shit she has no control over.

"Sorry," I mutter.

Red stops typing on the keyboard and turns slightly to look at me. "Don't be mad, okay? I just wanna get this out of the way now so we don't have to worry about it later."

I force a smile on my face and nod in agreement. Whatever makes her happy is what I'm always willing to do. I just wish it didn't involve Hoyt. That man was my hero for so many fucking years of my life, but the more time I spent under Millie's tyrannical roof, the more I began to hate everything and everyone.

Except for Red.

I could never find it in my heart to hate her, no matter how much I tried. We didn't start out as perfect friends; I just wanted to save the day and feel good about myself for once, because even as a kid, I knew I would never amount to anything for anyone. But she saw something in me and wouldn't let go of it, so neither did I.

"Babe, can you hand me my phone and earplugs, please?" I say to her as pleasantly as I can. She taps the keyboard a few more times before she gets up and disappears back toward the bedroom.

I chew my bottom lip while I wait for her to come back. I don't even bother looking at the laptop screen, because I don't have a say in these fucking plans, anyway. Red returns a few moments later and holds out what I asked her for. I let my eyes travel up her body before resting on her face, and smile.

"Thank you," I say sweetly, and watch as she blushes a slight shade of crimson and sits down again. "Well fuck, babe. You missed."

Red giggles nervously as she goes back to typing on her keyboard. At least she was able to have a positive reaction to my lame joke, which makes me feel slightly less bitter. I sigh as I plug my headphones into the jack on my phone and open up my music app.

Closing my eyes, I lay my phone on my chest and cross my other arm behind my head. *Black* by Pearl Jam comes on, and I begin to quietly hum along to the song. We've had a lot of good days to this particular tune, and a lot of bad ones, which makes it even more fortuitous that this happened to be the tune that plays first.

I have a special little playlist I keep handy for days like this. Days when Red is off in her own little world, fresh off a meltdown or a fuck, and it helps to keep me sane. It's not hard to deal with her mood swings as they come and go, but I find that if I immerse myself in the music of our youth, it makes them much easier to handle. Partly because I can tune her out, but mostly because eventually, I'll end up singing to her, and it puts her in way better spirits.

Red relaxes her body back against my legs, and I open one eye to glance at her. She's watching me with curious eyes—it's obvious she's asked me a question, and I completely missed it.

"What's up, babe?" I ask, pulling one of the plugs out of my ear.

"I was asking if you think our cars will make the trip, or if we should rent one," she repeats, biting her lower lip.

"Totally," I reply, placing the plug back in my ear. Red gives me a dirty look and turns her back to me again as she begins to type on the keyboard.

"We don't need to waste any more money, Red," I say in exasperation as I pull the plug back out again. "We'll take my car, and if anything happens to it, you know I can fix it, but we should be fine in the fucking car."

The look on her face immediately makes me regret how harshly I just spoke to her. I try to put my hand on her back, but she jerks her body away from me, picks up her laptop, and walks over to the love seat where she makes herself comfortable.

Alright, well, two can play this game.

I pick up my phone and quickly scan the list of songs until I find one that's always been a favorite of hers, turn on my side, and look at her. Her face is damn near buried in the screen, but when I start singing her favorite song, she glances up at me over the top and smiles slightly.

I stop and grin at her. "Want me to keep going, or are you gonna come over here and plant one on me?"

She rolls her eyes as she stands up with her laptop firmly in her hands, walks over, and kisses me gently on the lips. Of all the things I've ever experienced in this world, nothing ever compares to her lips against mine. Red's mouth is fucking magic, and she knows it, which makes situations like this a hell of a lot more tolerable when I have to coerce a little bit of lovin' out of her.

"I'm almost done," she says, settling down onto the floor in front of where I'm lying. I run a hand over the top of her head as she taps the keys a few more times, then shuts the machine down. "Okay, so I made the reservations for tomorrow night until Sunday, which means we should probably leave first thing in the morning."

"Tomorrow is Wednesday; why are we leaving two days early?" I ask her curiously.

"I don't know. I figure we can stop in Cold Spring for a little bit on the way. See if your tree house is still up in the backyard? It would be fun to check it out now we're adults, don't you think?" she asks, her eyes about a million miles away from here.

"That means we have to go to Millie's. Why the fuck would I want to go there?" I respond testily. She knows I've just come back from that shithole, and I wasn't in any rush to go back.

"Never mind," she replies quietly. "I just thought it would be fun. I'm sorry."

I let out a sigh and swing my legs off the side of the couch, careful not to kick her. "Babe," I start as I slide down onto the floor next to her, "I'm more than willing to go to Ossining. I will sit in the car for as long as it takes—I'll even drive the entire way there and back again, you know I don't mind driving, but I really don't want to go by Millie's if I don't have to."

Red nods, but turns her face away. I get it; I really do. She holds on to as many good memories as she can so she doesn't have to face the reality of the bullshit that was dumped on her as a kid, but there comes a point where I have to put my foot down, and Millie is definitely it.

"*Fine*," I reply through gritted teeth. "We can drive by it, but I'm not stopping the car. Will that be enough for you?"

She looks up at me with tears glistening brightly in her eyes and nods, a sad smile on her face. I blow out my breath and wrap an arm around her shoulder. It would have been nice to be able to have another go at her, but I'm used to putting my wants aside to make sure Red's okay. She's always done the same for me, with the exception of sneaking off to see Hoyt and not telling me.

I'll swallow my pride and get in that fucking car. I'll drive us all the way to death row and back again. I'll do it because it means the world to her to see him again, and I want her to have the world— even if I can't always give it to her with a smile on my face.

We're all each other has, and I plan on keeping her for as long as I can.

Uncle Jake's House, 1989

"Is Daddy coming back to get me?" I ask Uncle Jake quietly.

"He'll be back for you tomorrow, Gracie. Tonight, you get to sleep over," he replies with a smile creeping across his lips.

I sigh unhappily. Daddy had taken me to Millie's house, and as soon as he left, she started yelling at me, telling me that she didn't want me there. I didn't know where else to go, so I came to Uncle Jake's house.

I don't like being away from Daddy, and I don't much like being left alone with Uncle Jake. He likes to touch me a lot, but he gives me candy to keep quiet. When I start to cry, he stops and tells me he won't do it ever again if I can keep it a secret.

Liar, liar pants on fire, I think miserably. I sit by the big window in the living room and glance out into the night. I sure wish my friend Jori was with me. Everyone's scared of him—even a big guy like Uncle Jake. There was one time that Jori had come over to Momma and Daddy's house and they were arguing—well, Momma was yelling at Daddy, and he was just looking at her and letting her go like he always did, and he saw Uncle Jake trying to put my hand in his pants. He got so mad, he hit him as hard as he could, and told him if he ever saw him do something like that again, he'd bust his head wide open.

I told him it wasn't Uncle Jake's fault. It was mine, because I'm a dirty little girl like Momma always said, and you can't be mad at him for seeing what Momma saw. Jori told me that if it ever happened again, I had to tell him or he would make it a point to never speak to me. He's always been a good friend, but I didn't tell him again after that one time he saw it—he'd get into trouble for hitting Uncle Jake, and I don't want that for him.

"Gracie? Do you wanna sleep in my bed tonight, sweetheart?" Uncle Jake asks, coming over and putting a hand on my shoulder. "I'll take the couch tonight and you don't have to worry about … um … things. Your father was plenty pissed off, so I think you'll have enough to deal with in the morning."

I turn my face to look up at him. He knows something bad is gonna happen tonight—he knows it like I can feel it in my bones, and because of that, he's promising not to touch me, which is nice.

It'll be the first time in a long time he doesn't whisper to me that I'm sweet like a piece of candy while he's putting his hand in my underwear. I hate the way it feels, and his hands are always so hard and scabbed over—probably because he does the same work Daddy does, but so do I, and my hands aren't dirty or hard.

"Okay," I agree glumly. "You promise you're gonna stay out here?"

Uncle Jake bites his lower lip for a moment,

letting his hand run down my back before he pulls it away and nods. "I promise, baby girl."

I get up from the window and run up the stairs toward his bedroom, locking the door as soon as I get inside. I look around the room for anything I can push near the door to keep him out while I try to sleep. Almost everything is much too big for me to push by myself, but I do my best and pile up a bunch of bags he keeps in his closet against it. Then, I grab the chair he sits in when he tells me we're playing "candy store", and that's when he says that I have to "lick the lollipop".

I hate that chair—if I ever get the chance, I'm gonna smash it into a hundred pieces.

Once I'm pretty sure he can't get into the room, no matter how hard he tries, I climb into his big bed and pull the blanket up to my neck. It smells just like him and that usually doesn't bother me, because I've become used to his scent being on me a lot, but when he's not near me, it makes it worse.

It makes me feel like a dirty little girl, and I hate it.

I wanna go home. I miss Daddy and Jori, and I wanna go home.

I try not to cry, because if he hears me, he'll

come to see what's wrong, and I don't want him to come into the room. I want to be in here by myself, without having to worry about what he may try to do to me.

One day, things will get better. I'll be a grown up and he won't want to touch me anymore. He told me as much—he said he likes little girls but that I'm his favorite, so I should never be mad at him if he wants to touch anyone else.

I close my eyes tightly and think of Daddy. If I ever told him what Uncle Jake did, he'd probably hurt him real bad, and I don't want anything to happen to him either. Not because of me. No one should ever get in trouble because of me.

You're more trouble than you're fucking worth. That's what Momma always says to me when Daddy's not around, and I know she's only saying it because it's the truth.

I try not to let it bother me, because when I do get to be a grown up, I'm gonna run far away from home. I'm gonna get myself a car, and a 'partment, and I'm gonna leave this town and no one will ever see me again.

I think tomorrow when I see Daddy, I'll ask him if he'd like to go with me. We can take Jori with us too. The three of us can run away and we can be happy in a place of our own. I'll get a job so Daddy doesn't have to work anymore, and maybe a puppy to keep Jori company while I'm at work.

They'll be best friends, Jori and the puppy, and he'll get along just fine with Daddy, 'cause he says Daddy is his hero.

He's mine, though. I'll never find a friend as good as Jori, and even though Daddy should always be first in a little girl's heart, he doesn't know all the secrets I'm keeping from him. He doesn't know about the chair and the lollipop lickin'. I would never tell him that, but I would tell Jori, and maybe I will.

Maybe tomorrow, when Daddy comes to take me away from this bad place, I'll ask him if we can go to Millie's house and pick up Jori, and I'll tell him all the secrets I've been hiding from him. I'll ask him if we can run away now, and he'll say yes, 'cause he's my very best friend.

We'll come back for Daddy one day, and then the three of us will be happy again. We'll find a place where no one will ever be able to hurt us anymore. A place where I don't have to be alone with Uncle Jake. A place where Momma isn't yelling at Daddy, and a place where Jori isn't constantly fighting with Millie.

Yeah; tomorrow will definitely be a better day. It'll be a new start, and things will be so much brighter, just like the sun.

They have to be—they can't get any worse.

14

Present Day

"You about ready?"

I glance up from where I'm lounging on the couch and nod. Jori's standing in the kitchen with his arms crossed over his chest, car keys dangling from his hands, and a sour expression on his face, but he's ready to go.

I get to my feet and walk over to him, slide my arms around his waist, and look up into his eyes.

"Thank you. For coming with me," I say softly. He clears his throat and tightens his jaw. Nothing I can say to him will break him out of his shitty mood, and that's understandable, but it's because he thinks I'll make him stop at Millie's.

I won't.

I've decided it's not worth him being miserable on the trip back to Ossining.

"You're welcome," he finally replies with a sigh. "Let's get going."

We packed the car last night before we went to bed. Jori slept with his back to me, and that cut me deeper than I'll ever care to admit. I pull away from him and start walking toward the door, but he grabs me by the hand, stops me mid-stride, and turns me to face him.

Jori puts a hand on either side of my face and looks into my eyes. He's searching for something I can't quite figure out, but I'll let him look. There are only so many secrets I plan on being buried with, anyway.

"I love you. No matter what happens, I need you to remember that," he says quietly.

My body is threatening to melt under his touch and the fierceness of his words. I smile and gently rub my cheek against his hand.

"I love you too," I reply with a nod.

He looks down for a moment, before looking

THE LIES BETWEEN US

back into my eyes and nodding. Jori looks around the living room one last time, then leads me out of the house by my hand.

Something's bothering him, and he has no intention of telling me what it is. I feel like it's more than the possibility of having to see Millie again so soon looming over his head, but I'm not going to try and pry it out of him. If he tells me, he does; if he doesn't, it's not something I can dwell on for the sake of my own sanity.

Once we're outside, he locks the door and we head toward the car. Even though he's clearly in a pissy mood, he opens my door for me before he gets into the driver's side and sits down.

"Let's get this over with," he grumbles as he brings the car to life and pulls out into the street. I'm waiting for him to put his hand out palm up, but instead, he keeps his right arm rigid and hand firmly placed on the wheel. He opens his window and rests his elbow on the frame, keeping his eyes on the road in front of him.

We ride in silence for the first four hours of the trip. No music coming from the radio, no words exchanged, not even a spurt of road rage when someone cuts us off. Jori's car is great on gas, and he filled it before we left, so when he finally exits the freeway to find a gas station, I let out a sigh of relief. I'll go inside and find someone to talk to—even if it's just a hello. I need to hear a voice soon or I'll lose my shit.

We find a gas station about a mile down the road, and he pulls the car into an empty pump, then gets out without so much as a word. I wait for him to go inside and tell them how much gas he's putting in, and when he comes back out, I get out of the car and walk toward the convenience store doors.

I don't bother asking him if he wants anything because he probably won't even answer me. I'll just pick out some snacks and drinks and hope it's sufficient for now.

I power-walk toward the restroom. Four hours in a fucking car, and I need to go desperately. I'm surprised he hasn't had the urge yet, but anger can make all senses and functions shut down. That's something I know from personal experience.

Once I'm done in the restroom and my hands are thoroughly scrubbed clean, I head toward the aisle with the big bags of chips. He'll eat anything because he's a guy, and that's just how they are, so I don't spend too much time trying to decide what to get for him.

As soon as I've got a few choices picked out, I walk toward the back of the store where the coolers are and grab some bottles of water. I balance everything as best I can in my arms and head toward the front of the store, dumping everything onto the counter, smiling when I see the display of beef jerky bags just to the left of the register. I grab a couple and throw them onto the bags of chips and wait while my order is being rung up.

"Having a nice day?" I ask the girl behind the counter.

"It's going okay," she replies, with an indifferent shrug and zero eye contact. I sigh; maybe I should just stick to the silence—at least I know better than to expect any kind of friendliness if it's quiet.

"Um, that's seventeen dollars and twenty-two cents," she says, finally looking up at me. I nod and reach into my side pocket, pull out a twenty dollar bill, and toss it onto the counter. If she's not going to be friendly, neither am I.

As soon as she bags up my items, I collect my change from the counter and walk out of the store without so much as a "good-bye" or glance over my shoulder.

I don't like being mean to people, but I won't go

out of my way to be nice to someone who doesn't even care that I'm standing right in front of them.

I raise a hand to shield my eyes from the sun and walk toward the car. Jori's leaning on his side, one arm draped over the roof, watching me with a neutral expression carefully planted on his face.

"Are you all set?" he asks blandly.

I drop my hand from my face once I get to my side of the car and smile as best I can. Jori finally fucking laughs when my forced attempt at cheerfulness turns into a grimace.

"I got us some stuff," I say with a sigh, holding up the bag.

He shrugs, "Okay, well, let's keep going. Hell won't wait forever."

As he comes over to my side to open my door for me, something in me snaps and I swing the bag, hitting him squarely in the chest with it.

"Stop acting like a fucking baby!" I yell at him. "We don't have to drive by Millie's—fuck the tree house. I couldn't care less about it if that's what's got you in such a shitty mood. I just want to see my father again, 'cause Christ knows how many more visits I have left with him."

Angry tears stream down my face as he looks down at me in shock. There; I fucking said it. I finally admitted out loud that maybe *my* feelings should count for once instead of anyone else's, and that I know Hoyt's time is ticking.

It scares me.

Everything scares me, but never knowing when the last time I see him will be—not knowing when they'll sign his death warrant—became all too real for me when I saw him sitting on the other side of the thick glass window and I refuse to act like it doesn't hurt or bother me anymore.

"I'm sorry, Red," Jori says quietly, wrapping his arms around me and pulling me tightly against him. "I didn't mean to be such an asshole about this. I know you still love your old man, and you know he loves you too, right? We'll get there in a few hours, and you'll get to spend time with him again. It won't be the last time, and neither will be the time after that. Hoyt's got a long life ahead of him, I promise."

I let out a shuddering breath as I bring my hands up to his chest and gently push him away. Jori looks down at me and raises his eyebrows; he knows I have venom on the tip of my tongue right now, but I swallow it down and decide to speak from my heart instead.

"Don't make promises neither of us can keep," I

say sadly as I pull my door open and get into the car.

I don't care for gentlemanly theatrics right now. I just care about seeing Hoyt and trying to make up for the lost time we had. For all the years he spent trying to keep me away from the prison. I have to try to make it up to him somehow, and I have to tell him all the wonderful and terrible things I've held onto for far too long.

If anyone will understand what I've lived through, it'll be him.

Because even though he's Jori's hero, even though he's my second love, he'll always be the first man I turn to when I need to be saved from the terrible place that is the solace of my own mind.

15

Jori's not as angry as he was anymore. If anything, he's more talkative than ever before, and it's nice to be able to have a conversation right now. I'm not really listening to what he's saying, but I'm just happy words are finally coming from him that aren't laced with bitterness or anger.

I sigh and glance out the window. The closer we get to Ossining, the more nervous I become, and he can tell because he's finally reached for my hand.

"You alright, babe?" he asks curiously.

I nod and squeeze his hand. The truth is I'm not, and it's as obvious as the sky is blue, but I don't want to break him out of his good mood, so I'll swallow my fears and hope things will be okay this weekend.

"What's up, Red? Tell me," he says gently.

I take a deep breath and let it out in a long sigh. "I'm just scared, you know?"

"About what?" he prods carefully.

"That I lost too much time with Hoyt. That I never know if this will be the last time I get to see him or talk to him. That he'll tell me they've set the date and that there's nothing I can do about it," I ramble as my voice cracks.

I won't cry; not again. I've spent too many years crying because Hoyt kept turning me away when I asked to see him, but goddamn it—no matter what he's done, he's still my father.

"I honestly don't know if it will be, babe," Jori says slowly, "but I think the time you spend with him now means more to him than you think. And I'm sorry I was such a bastard with all of this. Cold Spring brings back a shit ton of bad memories for me, and I'm not dismissing that it does for you, too—please understand that. I just … I fucking hate that place so much."

"I know," I reply softly. I let go of his hand and lean over to lay my head on his shoulder. "That's why it means so much to me that you're here."

Jori clicks his tongue and nods sharply. He's trying to maintain his good mood, and I'm worried it won't last for too much longer if I keep talking.

"Thank you," I say softly, kissing him on the cheek before I lean back in my seat.

"You're welcome," he says, clearing his throat and reaching up into the visor above his head. "Here."

I look over and raise an eyebrow. He's holding out a cigarette—the one thing he absolutely hates that I do, yet he probably thinks it'll calm me down right now, and he's right.

I take it from him and push the lighter in the socket so it can start heating up, as he uses the buttons on his side of the car to lower my window. When the lighter pops out, I reach for it and hold it to the end of my cigarette, inhaling deeply. I'll be quick about it, since I know he hates this smell because it reminds him of Millie's house. Her voice became so damaged and her teeth turned a hideous shade of yellow due to how much she smokes.

I don't smoke very much anymore, and when I do, I tend to make sure I'm not near him.

I try to do my best to remember that I'm not the only one with shitty memories from childhood. Jori is great with it—he never plays the "my life was harder than yours" card, and he damn well sure can. I may have been through some hideous things, but I still had a mother and father, and at least one of them loved me.

Which is why he's on death row now.

Everything that happens in anyone's life is the direct result of an act on their part. I sometimes wonder how much better Hoyt's life would have been had I not been born. Hell, Jori may have had a better life without me too, but when those thoughts start to enter my head, I look over at him and think about how lucky I am.

Yes; things suck, life is hard, and not everyone gets dealt an easy hand, but to live the life that I have so far, and still find someone who cares about me as deeply as he does, makes every mental, physical, and emotional scar worth one miserable existence over a thousand deaths without him.

"What's the address of that hotel?" he asks, nodding at a highway sign. *Ossining, fifty miles.*

I take a shaky breath as I lean down and reach

for my purse that's sitting on the floor beside my feet. My hands are shaking as I pull out the paper, unfold it, and read him the information he asked for.

Jori nods and puts a hand on my leg. He gives it a gentle squeeze to let me know that he's still trying to stay in good spirits, but the closer to Ossining we get, the darker both of our moods become.

About an hour later, he's pulling off the highway and my entire life feels like it's caught up in my throat. As he slowly drives down the main road, looking for our street, I spot a drug store and get an idea.

"Hey, can you pull over?" I ask, pointing at it.

He nods as he clears his throat and checks the mirror. His jaw is tight and he's on edge—probably worried we'll run into Millie—but there's no reason for her to be in Ossining that I would know of.

Jori pulls into the parking lot behind the store and shuts the car off.

"I'll be right back," I say, reaching down for my purse and leaning over to give him a quick kiss. He nods and leans his chair back slightly, closing his eyes. He's probably tired after this trip, but I don't think we're too far away from the hotel at this point, anyway.

I walk through the sliding glass doors and look around before I see the aisle I'm looking for. Once I'm there, I take a look at the multitude of selections before me and can't help but wonder why there would be so many fucking brands just to do the same damn thing.

I finally decide on one and head back to the front of the store to wait in line. There's a woman in front of me with a little girl no more than six years old, and I can't help but smile. She looks so happy that her mother is letting her get a toy, and she's being reminded that it was for being a good girl all day.

When I was six years old, I felt a brush against the back of my head for the first time, and was told it was for being a disgusting animal no one ever wanted.

I know that little girl will have a good, happy life, and that makes me happy. I don't envy her for it, because unlike me, she deserves people who love and care for her.

"Miss?"

I look up curiously and blush when I see that

another register has opened and the young girl behind it is patiently waiting for me.

"Just this?" she asks, scanning my item.

I force a smile to my face and nod, as I set my purse down on the counter and retrieve my wallet. I pull out a twenty dollar bill and hand it to her without even waiting for the total. She takes the money and bags my item before she gets my change from the register and hands it to me with my receipt.

"Have a good evening," she says with a bright smile.

"You too," I reply softly as I slide my wallet back into my purse, grab my bag, and walk out of the store.

When I get to the car, I'm sure Jori's fallen asleep because I can see his chest evenly moving up and down as I approach. The moment he hears the door open, though, he sits up and smiles at me sheepishly.

"Sorry," he says with a yawn.

"Do you want me to drive the rest of the way?" I ask, hovering outside my door.

"No. I'm good. Got everything you need?" he asks, nodding at my bag.

"Yup. Shouldn't be too long now," I remark, sliding into my seat and closing the door.

He rubs his eyes tiredly before he turns the car back on and backs out of the parking spot. Once we're on the main road again, he's moving at a slow, steady pace, looking at the street signs as they go by.

"Ah! Left or right, babe?" he asks when he spots it.

"Um. Right, I think," I reply, glancing down at the paper again. "Yeah, right; the numbers should be going up this way."

We pass a few buildings before I perk up and squint my eyes at a sign halfway down the street.

"Over there," I say, pointing out a large brick building on his side of the road.

"Thank fuck," he mumbles, putting on his blinker and turning the car into the driveway of the hotel. He pulls the car to a stop in front of the office door, and I get out to go in and get us set up. I've got my bag with me because he can be nosy sometimes, and I don't want to have to explain myself with my latest purchase.

If he really loves me as much as he says he does, he'll understand when I show him what I've done.

It takes about twenty minutes to get checked

in, and once I have the room key, I thank the attendant at the front desk and head back outside. Jori is leaning against the car now, arms crossed over his chest, as he watches the cars go down the road.

"Got it," I say, holding up the key card and getting back into the car. "Go around the back— she said there's a door in the middle of the building back there that we can use."

Jori blows out his breath as he puts the car in drive and slowly creeps around the back of the building. I point out the first empty spot I see and he pulls in. I get out, holding my purse and bag tightly against my chest, and wait by the trunk for him. He shakes his head slightly and rubs his eyes again as he slides the key into the hole and unlocks the trunk. I reach for my bag, but he's faster, grabbing both of our weekend totes and slinging them over his shoulder.

"Lead the way," he says after he closes the trunk and nods at me as he slides his hands into his pockets.

We walk a few feet before we come across the door. I use the key card to gain access to the building, and hold the door open for him to walk through first. He smiles at me on the way in and waits patiently while I look at the number on the small envelope again.

"Should be just down the hall," I say as I begin walking.

Jori starts humming beside me as we make our way toward our room. I stop once I see number one fifty-five and pull the card back out of the envelope, slide it into the key slot, and push the door open for him.

He walks in and tosses the bags onto one of the empty beds and lies down, crossing his arms behind his head.

I smile at him as he watches me set my purse down. "I'll be back in a bit. I've got something to do."

He raises an eyebrow, but shrugs and reaches for the television remote, turning it on and cocking his head to the side so he can watch whatever program is on.

It should take about forty-five minutes to rid myself of Doreen Blackburn, and I hope he won't be too angry with me. I sigh as I put the bag down and take the box of hair dye out and rip the top off. I'm not too sure if this will work as well as I want it to, but if I can make it all black, I'll end up looking more like Hoyt, and make the visits with him more tolerable.

He shouldn't have to see Doreen anymore, and I shouldn't have to be subjected to looking even slightly like her because I have red hair.

With a sigh, I pull the gloves on and mix the contents together. Forty-five long minutes, and then I'll be a new person.

16

"Do you like it?"

I gasp and open my eyes. I had fallen asleep again, and I didn't even realize it. Rubbing my eyes, I turn to look at Red, who's looking at me, running a hand back through her wet hair and biting her lip anxiously.

"Holy shit," I say, sitting up.

Do I like it? I don't even honestly know what to think right now, because it bothers me to a certain extent that she changed her hair color, even though I know it's only because I'm not used to it. I'm sure as fuck not gonna start calling her Black, because she's my Red. Something tells me she's doing it to become a full-on Blackburn, and it honestly makes me sad to think this is the only way she knows how to rid herself of Doreen's memory, yet I know it'll make the visits with Hoyt easier on both of them.

"Babe, if this is what makes you feel better, then I'm all for it. You're beautiful, regardless of what your fucking hair color happens to be," I say, getting off the bed and walking over to her. She nods and looks away for a moment, so I take her face in my hands and lift it toward me.

I stare into her brown eyes and smile. She blinks a few times, more than likely trying to fight back some tears, and puts her hands on my wrists. I've never seen her look more vulnerable in her life, and it hits me harder than I thought it would. With as much shit as she's been through with her mother, her father, and her touchy-feely uncle, I would never expect that something like *my* approval of what she's done to herself would be the most of her concerns.

I lean down and press my lips softly against hers. I crave her kiss like she's craving my approval, and I refuse to let this moment pass without moving on it. I slide my tongue gently into her mouth and she meets mine in a wicked, seductive dance. She's making her wants clear right now, and I have every intention of giving her what she needs.

I let go of her face and slide my hands down her sides, reaching for her shirt and pulling it over her head. She pulls me back down to her, kissing me hungrily as she begins to pull the zipper on my pants down, snaking her hand in and grabbing my dick.

I gasp and pull away from her, but just for a moment. She's never been this bold with me before, and it's fucking intoxicating.

"Get on the bed," I say to her as I pull my shirt over my head. Red walks quickly past me, pulling down her shorts, then undoing her bra, letting them both fall to the floor. I ball up my shirt and toss it next to her clothes before I climb on top of her, hovering long enough to look into her eyes again.

She bites her lip as she sits up slightly. I move back and watch as she shimmies her panties off, exposing her pussy to me, and I lick my lips.

"Give me those," I say, holding out my hand. She hands them to me and lies back, waiting for me, but instead, I put them to my nose and inhale deeply. Everything about her—from the brown in her eyes to the smell of her cunt, is more than I'm worthy of, but she offers herself to me so freely, I'd be a fucking fool to ever deny her.

I run a hand down her naked body, looking at each inch I come in contact with, and furrow my brow. How I ended up with something as beautiful as this will always be a fucking mystery to me.

She's my special girl for as long as she'll have me, and I'll treat her as such.

My hand stops just above her pussy and I smile. Yeah; everything about her is fucking amazing, especially this.

I reach down and pull my pants and boxers off, and toss them over the side of the bed. I'll worry about where the fuck they went after, because right now, my girl needs to be tended to.

I move back over her and hold her wrists over her head. I'm already hard and ready to go, and I can smell how wet her cunt is, so all it's going to take to get this started is me sliding into what's mine.

She looks up at me with her innocent, big eyes, and I lean down to kiss her one last time as gently as I can. I let go of one of her wrists and reach down for my dick, place it against her pussy, and rub it against her. She squirms slightly and I smile.

"Keep your hands over your head," I whisper to her, as I lean down and kiss her neck. She nods and opens her legs a little wider as I grab onto her waist and slide my cock into her.

"Goddamn," I breathe, turning my head away as I keep pushing into her. She's always so fucking tight, no matter how many times we fuck, and it always feels like the first time with her.

"Ready?" I ask her in a thick voice. She nods, her eyes tightly shut, and I start to fuck her; gently at first, because it's always a work up to get her pussy to relax. I'm patient with it though, because I know how fucking amazing this always is, and once she's completely ready, she'll do whatever the fuck I want her to.

I take a deep breath and lean down over her, my hands on either side of her, as I begin to move faster. She lets out a loud moan and arches her back as I find a pace I know she'll be able to maintain.

Red keeps her hands over her head like I told her to, and the way her tits are bouncing while I'm slamming into her is fucking magic. There's never been a more beautiful girl in this world that I've laid eyes on, nor will there be. She's mine, and I'll protect her heart at all fucking costs.

"Are you still my dirty baby?" I ask her in a thick voice. The feeling of her pussy gripping my hard cock while I'm pushing into her is second only to her kiss. Red moves her grip to my forearms as she grits her teeth and nods, a whimper escaping from deep within.

"Good; get on your stomach," I command, pulling out of her and slapping her thigh. Red eagerly flips over, and as she does, I grab her hips and force her to keep her ass in the air. "Stay like this, or I'll have to hurt you way more than I know you can deal with."

I run a hand back through my sweat-slicked hair before I lean down and grab either side of her ass, sliding my tongue into her hole. She moans slightly and begins to play with her pussy, and the sound of how wet she really is greets my ears like a long, lost friend. I miss days when Red and I would just lie around the house and trade sexual favors for simple little things like trips to the fridge, who would have to get the remote, or even making bets, like the person who came first would end up cleaning up the mess.

I slide a thumb into her wet cunt and begin to

fuck her with it as she rubs her clit faster and moans louder. I pull my mouth away from her ass and a wicked smile creases my lips. I can't remember the last time she was so eager for a dirty fuck, and I'm more than happy to oblige my pretty baby. I slick my other thumb with my tongue, a nice loud sucking sound so she knows what's coming, before I slide it into her tight asshole and begin to fuck both of her holes vigorously. She lets out a yelp and attempts to push my hands away, but I use my knee to open her legs wider and make it easier to fuck her with my thumbs.

"Oh my god," she breathes. "I can't—Jori, stop!"

"Oh yes fucking you can," I reply through gritted teeth. "And if you're a good dirty baby for me now, maybe next time it'll be another dick instead of just my hands."

I've never thought in a million years I'd offer to let her fuck more than just me, but I can tell she's enjoying it, no matter how much she's bitching about it. I watch as she grips the bed sheet with her fists and attempts to push herself up. I pull my thumbs out of her and use a hand to push her head firmly back down onto the pillow.

"I didn't tell you you could move, Red. Keep your ass in the air and hang on tight, baby," I direct as I position myself behind her. I grab her by the hips and spit into the palm of my hand, slicking my dick as best I can before I begin to slide it into her ass. We've done this maybe once or twice before, but she's never lasted very long because of how tight she is. Tonight is gonna be different, though—she's not gonna stop until *I* say we're done, and she'll thank me for it.

I don't force my dick into her; that'd be a sure-fire way to fuck this up and hurt us both. I'm gentle with the way I slide into her ass, and once I'm in and her hole is clenched tightly around me, I begin to slowly move in and out of her. Her body will relax soon enough, and then I'll fucking destroy her. It's how she knows I love her—the harder I fuck her, the deeper in love with her I fall, and her with me.

She lets out a pained gasp as I begin to push into her a little faster. Then, when she's as used to the feeling of my dick inside her as she can be, she reaches back and grabs hold of my balls.

"Fuckin' right," I breathe as I begin to fuck her faster. Red's moans—the pain in her breathing—there's not another sound in the world that can compare to it, and it's just for me to hear.

I smack the side of her ass and reach down for

a handful of her new black hair, arching her back toward me. She lets go of my balls now, because she's too little to reach them in this position, and begins to play with her pussy again. She's going to come soon, I can tell by the way she's breathing, the way her moans are getting louder.

"Jori..."

The way she gasps my name, the way her ass jiggles each time I slam into her—it's becoming too much for me.

"Come on, dirty baby. Come for me, you know you want to," I say, pulling her back closer to me. She reaches a hand back and grabs my arm as she keeps playing with her wet cunt.

"Oh fuck!" she yells, and I close my eyes, grind my teeth together, and come deep inside her ass. Red is still working her pussy, and even though it won't be long now, I have no intention of letting her get herself off.

"Fuck that," I growl, slapping her hand away and turning her onto her back. I take a deep breath and shake the euphoria away as I open her legs widely and slide her down toward me.

I slide my tongue up her slit before I begin sliding a finger in and out of her damp hole. Red is squirming on the bed as she grabs my hair and pulls hard. I smile for a moment, but once I start licking and sucking on her clit, I don't let up. This belongs to me, and she knows it.

"*Ugh,*" she moans loudly, arching her back one last time and pulling my hair as hard as she can. I flatten my tongue as the warm juices of her pussy flow out, and make damn sure I can taste every last drop of her before I lick her clean and finally look up at her.

She runs a hand over her face and lets out a laugh, glancing down at me still between her legs, and I grin.

"Feeling better?" I ask, tilting my head to the side.

"*Much,*" she replies with a lazy smile.

"Good."

I pull myself up on the bed and move to the side of her, slide an arm around her waist, and hold her close. I can't get rid of everything plaguing Red, but at least I was able to take her mind off it for a while.

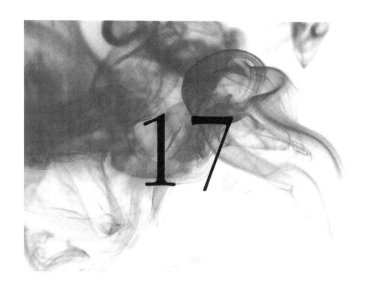

Blackburn Residence, 1989

I can hear them screaming at each other, and it's kind of scary. I've never known Hoyt to raise his voice before, but he's really pissed off tonight. After Millie chased Red away, I came running over here to see if she had come back home, 'cause I was gonna take her back to my tree house if she did.

I sneak over to the window and look inside. For once in her life, Doreen looks scared of Hoyt, and I can see why. His face is bright red and he's got her backed into a corner.

I should probably leave and get some help, but I wanna see what's gonna happen, so I reach my slender fingers under the window sill and bring it up just enough that I can hear what's going on inside.

"How long have you been doing this? Don't fucking lie to me!" he screams at her.

I jump.

He's definitely a different person when he's angry, and I'm glad Red isn't here to see it, 'cause she doesn't need to be scared of her dad, too—she's got enough people to be afraid of.

"I don't know what you're talking about!" Doreen screams back at him.

"You fucking bitch—I'll fucking kill you, I swear to God," he seethes, taking another step toward her.

I bite my lip and slide the window back down. If he wants to get rid of Doreen, I'm gonna help him. I don't like the way she treats Red and how she's always hitting her and sending her to Jake's house. She knows what he does to her, 'cause Red told her once and she told her to shut her mouth about it.

I can feel myself getting angry so I'm gonna put it to good use. I creep around the side of the house, making sure I'm hidden in the shadows until I get to the back door, and turn the handle upward instead of down. They don't know it, but I've been sneaking into their house whenever I can to get Red. I always bring her back before the sun comes up, but I just like being around her and I know how to make her smile when she's crying.

She's someone who likes having me around, and I've never had that before. She's my best friend, and I'm not gonna let anyone hurt her ever again.

I quietly walk into the kitchen and close the door behind me. Hoyt's yelling has calmed down some, and it's Doreen's turn now. She's screaming at him like she has a right to be mad. Like *she's* the one who's been getting beaten, touched by her uncle, and having a bunch of bad words thrown at her.

My eyes glance around the kitchen counter and I smile when I see a meat hammer sitting on a cutting board next to a big slab of beef. It looks like Hoyt interrupted her in the middle of making dinner, but she doesn't need to worry about finishing anymore.

I walk over and grab it, then make my way to the living room, where they're having their fight. I gasp and move back a little when Hoyt suddenly walks down the hall, and I'm worried he's seen me, but when he doesn't turn around, I know he hasn't.

I crouch down behind the door frame and wait until he comes back a few moments later. He's a blur of anger and dark clothes, his boots heavy on the wooden floor as he disappears back into the living room. I think I saw him holding a box, but I'm not too sure 'cause he moved so fast.

"I'm going to collect my child," he says to Doreen quietly. "You can have this fucking house and everything in it, but you're never seeing Gracie again."

Panic goes through me like a shock wave. If he takes Gracie and leaves, that means I'll never see her again, either, and that's not fair! I didn't do anything to her for him to take my best friend away!

With a grunt of pure rage, I run out from the kitchen, into the living room, and straight to Doreen. She loses her footing and falls back down on the couch 'cause she wasn't expecting anyone else to be in the house.

I raise the hammer over my head and bring it down onto her skull as hard as I can. She lets out a scream, but I hit her again and again until she's gurgling and her eyes start to fix on the wall behind me.

"Jori!"

Hoyt grabs me by the shoulders and pulls me off her, wrestling the hammer out of my hand. It's hard to breathe when I'm this angry, but if Doreen is gone, Red can stay here.

"I'm not done," I shout, trying to wriggle out of his grip, but he's a heck of a lot stronger than I am.

"What did you do?" he yells, turning me to face him and shaking me by the shoulders. "What the fuck did you do?"

"You were gonna leave. You were gonna take Red with you, and I was never gonna see her again, and she's the only person who cares about me," I shoot back, hot tears rolling down my cheeks. "You can't take my best friend away!"

Hoyt pulls me toward him and puts an arm around me, the hammer resting against my back. He's breathing really fast right now, but I think it's 'cause now, he's scared of *me.*

I wipe away the tears angrily and look up at him. I don't care if Doreen dies; I don't care if he hates me for the rest of my life, but Red is staying with me.

He takes a deep breath and lets it out in a long rush.

"Okay. Okay; take this box and get out of here. I'll take care of this," he says, nodding at Doreen behind me. She's not making any more sounds, so I think she's gone to sleep now, but when she wakes up, she'll know better than to mess with Red again. She'll know I'm not scared of her, and I'll beat her up worse next time if she tries it.

Hoyt shoves the box into my hands, puts a hand on top of my head, and looks into my eyes for a moment.

"Go home, Jori. Make sure you take good care of my baby for me, okay?" he says, a tear rolling down his face. "Everything you'll need for a while is in there, and I don't want you to ever tell Gracie what happened here tonight, understand?"

I nod, even though I don't.

"Leave your shirt here; I'll get rid of it," he says, holding out his hand. I place the box on the table for a second to pull my shirt off and hand it to him, and when he takes it, a sad smile crosses his face.

"Gracie's lucky to have a friend like you."

I square my shoulders back proudly and take one last look at Doreen's sleeping body. Her bones are sticking out of the half of her face I can see, and I think I can see some of her teeth on the floor. I tilt my head to the side for a second or two, and stare just a little bit longer. If Hoyt hadn't stopped me, I bet I could have made her look like that half beaten meat on the counter.

I almost forget he's standing behind me until he gives me a gentle nudge and I grab the box and run out the front door.

I'm not sure what Hoyt's gonna do, but I'm sure I'll find out tomorrow when I come check on Red. As my shoes slap the pavement and I run back home as quickly as I can, I know things will be okay. He won't get into too much trouble though, 'cause he didn't do anything wrong.

It was me.

18

Present Day

The bed is empty the next morning when I wake up, and I hate that feeling. It's utter loneliness in a world where I already feel alone enough.

I let out a sigh as I push myself off the side of the bed and notice that the door to the hallway is slightly cracked. I don't understand why he didn't just take a key card with him, but I walk over to the desk and slide my feet into his flip-flops.

Once I locate one of the keys, I look into the large mirror sitting behind the television, and smile slightly. I definitely look more like Hoyt now with the black hair, and I may end up keeping it.

Running my hands back through my hair, I leave the room and pull the door closed behind me. Once it clicks, I head down the hallway and out the back doors. I have to shield my eyes from the morning sun and look around for a few seconds, but I finally see him sitting down on the ground a few feet away from the car. His arms are draped over his knees, and he just seems to be watching the cars go by.

He's got on a white basketball top and black gym shorts, barefoot, and he still somehow manages to look so fucking sexy that I feel my heart fluttering as I walk over to him.

"Morning," I say as I get closer.

Jori turns his head slightly and smiles at me, lifting his face for a kiss when I get next to him. I lean down and press my lips softly against his before I sit down and lean my head against his shoulder.

"Morning, babe. You sleep okay?" he asks, looping an arm around me and pulling me closer. I reach for his other hand and lace my fingers through his, nodding.

"Yeah; I'm okay," I reply.

"Good. So what did you want to do today?" he asks.

"Nothing, really. Maybe look around? I didn't get to do that the last time I was here," I say with a shrug.

"Is there even anything to do in this Podunk town?" he asks with a scoff.

"Why, Jori Davidson, when did you become such a ray of sunshine?" I tease, glancing up at him with a smile on my face.

He chuckles and looks away. "Honestly Red, I'd be just fine with staying in the room until tomorrow."

"And do what?" I ask, making a face at him.

"I don't know. We can just lie in bed and watch TV," he replies with a shrug, pulling his arm and hand away. "And if we get bored ... well ..."

I roll my eyes and giggle when he nudges me suggestively. "Aren't you tired? How do you possibly have that much energy?"

"Have you seen yourself, Red? How could I not? Besides, if you're not up for it again, you know I'm always hungry," he replies with a sly smile on his face.

"Oh Jesus," I reply with a laugh as I get to my feet. I kick his flip-flops off my feet and nod at them. Jori rolls his eyes and slides them on, getting up and crossing his arms over his chest.

"Anything else, *Mom?*" he teases with a grin.

I take a step back, looking him up and down. The white of his shirt makes the colorful art on his arms stand out, and the black in his shorts somehow manages to do the same thing for his legs. I know there's no such thing as perfect, but I swear he's the closest I've ever seen anybody come to it.

"Alright, go get yourself washed up and we'll go out and grab something to eat. I'm getting hungry again, and I don't wanna eat this hotel shit," he says, slinging his arm around my shoulder and walking me back toward the doors. "I'll be in soon."

I narrow my eyes at him and he laughs. "I'm not doing anything bad, Red. All the bad things I wanna do have always involved you, anyway," he says with a wink, sticking the tip of his tongue out suggestively.

I throw my hands up in the air and walk back into the building. The doors don't lock during the day, so I let it slam behind me, his laughter still following me until I get a few doors down.

I hope he plans on taking a shower before we

go anywhere, because he definitely needs one. I won't mention it to him, though, because I don't want him to think I'm being bossy or catty; I just don't think anyone else wants to smell the sweat and sex lingering on him.

Once I get to the room and the door is left slightly ajar for him, I walk over to my bag and pull out some fresh clothes and underwear before I head to the bathroom.

I quickly undress and fold my shirt and shorts neatly, placing them on the vanity before I slide off my panties and slip them in between. The room is quickly steaming up, and that makes me smile because I know the water is already up to a temperature I'll be comfortable with.

Pulling back the curtain, I step a foot in to test the water, then immerse myself in the stream completely. It feels nice to have a hot shower that's nothing more than a moment to clean myself off. I don't feel so dirty when I'm this close to Hoyt, because in a really fucked up way, I feel like he can still protect me from all the bad people in the world.

Besides, I don't wanna go see him with patches of hair missing, or scratches on my arms—I'm sure he has more than enough shit to deal with; he doesn't need to see that his daughter is all fucked up in the head on top of everything else.

Closing my eyes, I turn my body away from the torrent and lean my head back, running my hands through my hair. I'm sure some of the black will run out of it because I didn't do enough of a good job last night at getting it all out. I didn't even notice that until I saw the black stains on the sheets, so if anything else, we'll have to stop some-where and buy some cheap ones to replace the ones I've ruined.

I reach for the mini shampoo bottle with my eyes still closed, and laugh when my hand hits a barrier made of flesh and bone.

"Didn't think I'd pass this up, did you?" Jori asks, placing his hands on my sides.

"Behave," I instruct him, opening one of my eyes. "It's shower time, and that's it."

He grunts and turns around, reaching for the shampoo, popping it open with his thumb, and tells me to hold my hand out. He squeezes half the bottle into the palm of my outstretched hand, then pulls his hand away from me to put the rest in his, and sidesteps me.

"Um, can I have some water? It's shower time, after all," he says, making a face at me.

I giggle as I begin to lather up my hair. This tiny bottle definitely isn't enough for the both of us, so I'll pick some up while we're grabbing the sheets, too. Jori leans his head to the side and opens one eye. When he catches my attention, he promptly sticks his tongue out, then closes his eye again, turning his back to me.

I laugh and playfully slap him on the back.

"Ooh. Careful; you don't wanna get me all worked up now, do you?" he asks, turning his head to glance at me from the corner of his eye. I watch the water as it trails down his back, dancing along the huge tattoo that's watching me just as carefully as he does sometimes, and smirk.

"I could slap you in the face and it would get you all worked up," I reply with a chuckle.

Jori laughs and turns back around to face me. "Pass me the soap, babe?"

I turn around and reach for the bar and begin picking at the wrapper until I pull it off and hand it to him.

A slow smile begins to spread across his face as he rubs the bar quickly between his hands, then begins to deliberately rub it over his chest. His eyes never leave me, the smile never disappears, as he moves it lower on his stomach and I watch the water with envy, because it's touching every inch of his body like I'm aching to.

I don't give in, though. Instead, I bite my lip and look away, because if I don't, I'll need to take a shower to recover from this one. He laughs and holds the soap out, which I reach out and take, making sure not to look him in the eyes as I do.

"Too much walking shoes worn thin ..." he begins to sing as he turns away from me again, letting the water wash the soap off his body.

I take the opportunity to turn away from him and quickly rub the soap all over my skin. If I can just get this done before he turns around and sees me partially bent over, I can get out of this shower unscathed.

"Well, hello there," he says gently, as he reaches forward and grabs my hips, pressing himself against me.

"Jori. Not now. Please?"

He lets out a sigh and immediately releases his grip. The sound of his hands slapping his thighs tells me he's slightly pissed off, but he'll get over it.

The curtain whips open and stays that way as he reaches for a towel and wraps it around his waist. He glances at me in the mirror and I give him a dirty look as I pull it closed again, washing the rest of the soap off. I stand under the torrent for a few more seconds to make sure the shampoo is out of my hair, then turn the faucet off.

When I pull the curtain open, he's leaning against the vanity with his arms crossed, watching me with a carefully indifferent look on his face.

"Are you okay?" I ask him curiously as I step past him and reach for the spare towel. I bring it up and wrap it around my chest, securing it in place, before I place my hands on my hips.

"Yeah. Why wouldn't I be?" he quips with a forced smile on his face. I sigh and reach for him, letting him pull me into his arms, and I close my eyes.

Eventually, he'll tell me what the big deal is, and why he really hates being so close to Cold Spring. For now, I just want to live blissfully unaware of what's going on in his head, and go grab a bite to eat.

Sing Sing Correctional Facility
3 Years Ago

My leg hasn't stopped shaking since I sat down in this fucking chair. I'm pretty sure I've chewed my thumbnail down to the quick, and I pull my hand away from my face, spitting out the bits of nail I've managed to chew off.

I don't know why I'm really here right now. I mean, I do, but I don't know if I'm fully prepared to get the answers I'm looking for. Unfortunately, the only person who's going to be able to give me the honest to god's truth is Hoyt Blackburn.

I'm more here for my Red than anything else, because she can't take any more fucking blows than life has already dealt her. I want to take some of this shit off her shoulders—even if it means putting myself in a fucking state I won't be able to claw my way out of.

And if I'm right, if Hoyt confirms what I found, I'll keep it from her for as long as I can. I almost lost her once a long fucking time ago, and I won't risk it again. Bad things tend to happen when I'm faced with losing Red, and there are only so many people left to take my anger out on before it turns to her. I'll never let that happen, though. I'll turn all my fucking rage onto myself before I ever hurt her.

I sigh and irritably run a hand back through my hair. I've been staring at the door on the other side of the thick glass window for so goddamn long, I feel like my eyes are gonna dry up and turn to dust if it doesn't move soon.

Leaning back in my chair, I blow out my breath and look at the painfully white wall next to me. It makes me hope that the rest of this prison isn't the exact same mind-numbing color. I'm sure it could be enough to drive any man crazy. It's starting to agitate me, and I've only been in here for about ten minutes.

Just when I'm ready to give up and leave, I can hear a pair of voices on the other side of the door. I sit up and arch an eyebrow as the door opens. I haven't seen Hoyt in *years*, but he doesn't look too different from what I remember. I'm pretty sure that, standing, he's still got an inch or two on me, but that's about it.

As soon as he's out of his chains and our eyes lock, I pick up the phone receiver on my end and wait for him to do the same thing. Instead, he just sits down and stares at me for a moment, drumming his fingertips along the countertop.

Hoyt shakes his head slightly before he finally picks up his phone and holds it to his ear. I open my mouth, but he shakes his head, and almost imperceptibility raises his eyes to the camera in the room above me.

I get it; we're being recorded. They can hear everything we say, and they can see everything we do. I understand he's just being careful, but we're past that shit now.

I nod once just to let him know I'll watch what I say, and he leans back in his chair, receiver pressed against his ear, and waits.

"How ya doing, old man?" I ask him quietly.

"About as good as I can be, I guess," he replies with a shrug. His voice is just as deep as I remember it, and the little boy in me smiles, because he's talking to his hero again. The man in me keeps a straight face and a hardened heart, because if he ever truly was my hero, he wouldn't have let things go this far.

"What can I do for you, Jori?" he asks, leaning forward and placing his elbows on the counter. The way he asks me—it's almost as if he thinks he actually *can* do something for me, locked up in a prison. "Is it Gracie? Is she okay?"

"Red's fine," I reply curtly. He nods and I clear my throat. I'm not entirely sure how to go about this, and it's not exactly something to just blurt out. "Uh … I've got a couple of things I need to talk to you about."

Hoyt's unnerving eyes never waiver as he glances up at the camera again, then back at me with a nod.

"How's that box doing? Half full or half empty?" he asks, with a soft smile.

"More than half full," I reply, picking nervously at the chipped counter. "We don't need much, you know? I'm really careful with how much we spend out of it, because I don't want to leave her alone for eight hours a fucking day just to make ends meet."

I instantly cringe at my choice of words. That box held Hoyt's life savings from the day he started working when he was fourteen years old, up until he got arrested for Doreen's murder. That shit still eats at me—he put his prints all over that fucking hammer and burned my shirt to ash before he called the cops and turned himself in over a crime he didn't commit. All because a twelve year old boy was scared of losing his best friend—that's the hero in him, but that's not who I'm looking for right now.

Hoyt chuckles into the receiver. "Good. I'm glad to know you kids are still doing okay … you know, with my eight hours a day away from Gracie," he teases.

"Sorry. Shitty choice of words," I mumble, looking down at the counter. I wouldn't mind getting a job. It would be nice to get out of our place for a change, but I just can't fathom leaving her alone for that stretch of time, five days a week. I would feel like I'm abandoning her.

"So what's on your mind?" he asks again, curiously.

I turn my eyes back up toward him, leveling an even stare through the glass. "Why didn't you tell the truth?"

Hoyt shakes his head and holds up a warning finger. "I won't talk about that. If that's what you're here for, I'll have to go."

I bite my lip angrily and grip the receiver tighter. There's only one more piece of truth I'm here for, and it's going to fucking break me if he confirms it.

"Alright," I begin as I clear my throat. "I found a large envelope at the bottom of the box—under the money? I ... uh ... I opened it and I read what was inside, and—" My words catch in my throat as venomous tears spring to my eyes, and I stare at him, waiting for him to confirm or deny my findings.

A sad smile forms on Hoyt's tired face and he looks down at his hands for a moment.

"Oh my God. Goddammit," I breathe, looking down and shaking my head. The receiver falls from my hands as the tears continue to fall. Hoyt knocks on the glass a few times until I finally look up, and motions for me to pick the receiver back up.

"I want you to listen to me, okay?" he begins gently. "I ..." He sighs. "Me and Doreen were never officially married. We referred to each other as husband and wife because of that common law bullshit, but I did love her like she was mine on paper, you know? Anyway, she never wanted kids, but I didn't know that until after. I thought that if we gave you to Millie for a while, she'd come around, and at least I could go and visit with you. But I guess my sister was as bitter as Doreen's brother was a fucking whack job, but I didn't know that until after everything happened."

"Why do we have different last names?" I ask him, my voice shaking.

"Doreen's maiden name is Davidson. She wouldn't let me in the room when you were born, so I fought her tooth and nail for Gracie's name. I never *not* wanted you; you're my boy. I've loved you even when I wasn't allowed to go near you, and that's the reason why, to answer your first question. I've never been able to do shit for you your entire life, but I was able to do this, and I jumped at the chance to fucking be a good father to you when the opportunity came up."

"Um, does Red know?" I ask him, closing my eyes and covering my face with my free hand.

"No. She never knew you were her brother. To be honest, it made me happy to see you two getting along so well, you know? It's almost like deep down inside, you both knew something was different about the other one, yet still the same," he replies with a wistful laugh.

My lower lip is trembling to the point where the sob will escape me soon if I don't get it together. The girl I love above everyone else on this rancid planet ... there's been a reason the entire time, but it never clicked with either of us.

"Hey," Hoyt suddenly says in an even tone. "How close exactly are you two, anyway?"

I meet his eyes again and put a fist to my mouth to keep from outright bawling. A look of understanding washes over his face as he leans back in his chair.

"Fuck," he mutters quietly. Hoyt turns his face away for a moment to compose himself before he looks at me again. "Listen to me. I can forgive you for what happened before today because you didn't know, but I cannot and *will not* forgive you for anything that happens when you leave this room. Do you understand me?"

I nod and use my knuckles to wipe away my tears. I have one more question for him, and then I'll walk away and never think of him again.

"Do you think her life would be better if you were still in it instead of me?" I ask him quietly.

"That's tough to say, Jori," he replies, shaking his head. "I don't know how many more years I've got left—on the inside or outside. You're still a young kid in your twenties, and as long as you keep your head on straight, you'll probably be around a hell of a lot longer than I would be, anyway."

I nod and blow my breath out. Hoyt just sealed his own fate, because had he said himself, I would have stopped at the front desk and turned myself in for the murder of Doreen Davidson.

"Alright. That's all I wanted to know; thanks," I say, getting to my feet and hanging up the phone.

Hoyt taps the glass again to get my attention, but I walk out without so much as a backward glance. Once I get back to the car and back onto the road, I'll light my birth certificate on fire, and Red will never know that we shouldn't be together the way we are.

She'll love me for being the man by her side, instead of the brother she didn't know she'd been growing up with all along, and it'll be okay, because once Hoyt's dead, there will be no one left to tell her, anyway.

Present Day

With the shopping out of the way, Red seems to be in better spirits. She made such a big deal about being charged too much for the sheets that I just smiled and let her ramble on until we got to the register. That's when she remembered she hadn't grabbed any shampoo bottles or extra soap.

When she came back to the front of the store, she seemed embarrassed that I'd held up the line, but I wasn't going to wait in the back when I knew she was returning.

Besides, I was fucking hungry, and was starting to get agitated because of it. But that was all a half an hour ago, and now we're sitting in a rustic little place, by the window, watching the world go by as we eat. I like seeing her happy; it's a rare thing to see a genuine smile on her face when we're outside of our home. Usually, we both look sulky and discontent, but I think being this close to Hoyt again has her spirits up.

"I wanna ask you something," she suddenly says, putting her fork down and folding her arms on the table. I glance at her, still chewing on my steak, and arch an eyebrow.

"What's up, babe?" I ask once I'm done chewing. I stab another piece of the meat and pop it into my mouth as I wait for Red to say what's on her mind.

She smiles at me and it makes me feel better because, for some reason, her staunch silence after getting my attention had set me on edge for a minute.

"Do you ever see yourself with someone else? Besides me, I mean?" she asks as she adjusts an arm and drops her chin into her palm.

"Never," I reply immediately. "Next question."

She lets out a girlish giggle as she picks up her

fork and cuts off another piece of her chicken parmesan.

I don't know why the hell that thought would ever cross her mind, but now, I want to know.

"Why would you even ask me that?" I ask, looking at her curiously. I'm gripping my fork so tightly right now that I could snap the fucking thing in half if I wanted to, but the longer she takes to answer me, the more apprehensive I can feel myself becoming.

Maybe being this close to Hoyt is doing wonders for Red, but it's fucking with me in a completely different way. I let out a breath I didn't even realize I was holding, and drop my fork with a loud clatter onto the plate. I reach for my water and take a swig, before damn near slamming the glass back down onto the table. I lean back and cross my arms over my chest, waiting for her to answer me, but she's lost in her own little world right now, of chicken and thoughts of a different man in her life.

"Red. What the fuck? Why did you ask me that?" I ask her in a sterner tone than I mean to.

She looks up at me, her face clouded in confusion. "It was just a question, Jori."

I clench my jaw tightly and look at her for

another moment before I pick up my fork and knife, and cut another piece of steak. I've lost my fucking appetite, but I don't want her to realize it or she'll know she's pissed me off.

The one thing I always promised myself with her was to never stay mad at her longer than it takes to finish a meal. She's had enough people treat her like shit in her life—she doesn't need it from me, too.

"Okay," I reply as indifferently as I can, putting the steak into my mouth. The more I chew it, the staler it's starting to taste, but I'm going to eat this entire fucking plate, and she'll think nothing is wrong.

That's the only thing that ever matters to me. I'll swallow all my shit and keep it bottled up as long as Red has a better life now than she did as a kid.

"Hey," she says, reaching a hand across the table and resting it on my forearm. "I'm sorry if I upset you. It really was just a question."

I clear my throat, swallow the bit of stale shit in my mouth, and shake my head. "I'm fine, babe. I promise. See?"

I turn my eyes away from the window and force a grin on my face. Red smiles slightly and shakes her head, giving my arm a squeeze. I raise an eyebrow at her before I lower my face quickly and take a gentle bite of her hand. She leans back with a smile on her face before letting go, satisfied that all is well for now.

My stomach is turned and my taste buds have gone rotten. It amazes me how something as simple as her thinking I would ever want or need anyone besides her has fouled my mood so much.

"Are we going back to the hotel after we're done here?" I ask, in an attempt to change the subject.

She nods, "We can. It'll give me time to get rid of those sheets and put the new ones on the bed."

I shake my head and chuckle. She's not gonna get a moment's peace until she swaps out those fucking sheets, and that's okay. If that keeps her mind off the random bullshit, I'll stand there and watch her change the damn things.

Maybe she'll let me have another go at her, maybe she won't, but I'm gonna try for it. Her happy place seems to be clean beds and a full stomach, while mine is anywhere I can be near or inside of her.

Red finishes up her meal and pats her stomach. "Food baby," she says with a happy sigh.

I tilt my head to the side, a smile crawling across my lips as a thought enters my mind. It's not the first time I've had it, but it's the first time I'm ever speaking it.

"Maybe one day, I can put a real one in there," I suggest nervously as I reach for my glass of water.

She blinks rapidly a few times and sits straight up. The thought isn't lost on her, and I can tell she's weighing the option. It makes me nervous when she doesn't answer right away, but when her eyes soften and she nods her head slowly, I let out a sigh of relief.

"Yeah; maybe. I think we'd be good parents, you know?" she says wistfully.

"Better than what we got dealt, that's for sure," I agree, setting my glass back down. "Alright, do you see our server? I wanna get the check so we can get out of here. I'm sure those sheets are burning a hole in the back seat," I tease with a wry smile.

Red reaches for her purse and I shake my head as I fish my wallet out of my pocket. "I got it, babe."

She nods and sets it down, leaning back in her chair and glancing out the window. I let my eyes linger on her for a few seconds; they say staring at the sun is bad for your eyes, but when something shines so fucking brightly, how can you help but look at it?

I cut my gaze toward the server as she approaches and asks us if we're all set. With a nod, I ask her for the check, and she says she'll be back with it shortly. Red's still staring out the window, and I'm still stealing glances at her when I can.

"Here you go. You two have a nice day!"

Red turns her face to smile at the server, then tries to crane her neck to see how much our bill is, but I pull it away from her prying eyes.

"Relax, kid," I say with a laugh as I slide three ten dollar bills inside and get to my feet. "If you spend all your time worrying how much the food cost, you're not gonna have enough energy to make the bed."

She makes a face at me as she retrieves her purse from the seat next to her. I wait patiently by the side of the table for her, then put an arm around her shoulders as we begin to walk out of the place.

Tomorrow will be harder than today, but as long as the sun still shines brightly in my arms, there's nothing we can't deal with.

Millie's House, 1992

Jori's been gone for days with no mention that he was leaving, let alone where he would be going to. I've been sneaking around his room looking for clues. I waited till Millie was gone though, 'cause if she could be downright nasty to me when he's around, I'm afraid to think of how she could be if we were alone.

It makes me sad to think that he would leave me behind in this place without a friend anymore, but if I can just find something, *anything,* that might tell me where he went, it just might tell me if he's coming back, too.

There's nothing out of the ordinary that I can find. His room has always been a little messy, yet we both seem to know where everything is when we need it. *All I need right now is the one thing that's not in this room,* I think with a sad sigh as I drop down onto his bed.

I put a hand over my face and think about the days when all I wanted in the world was my daddy. He would come from hard days at work and have a smile on his face, and a big, warm hug for me, no matter how tired he was. When the cops took him, I was so confused, because I knew Daddy could have never hurt Momma, no matter how much she deserved it. I cried for weeks about it, and when I felt like my heart would just burst from all the sadness, Jori was always there to make sure I still had a big, warm hug to fall into.

He made a promise to me the day they came for Daddy—no matter how bad the world would ever seem to me, he would never leave me behind. He promised to stay by my side until I said I didn't need him anymore, but I don't ever see that day coming, and it's nice to have a best friend like him.

It's nice to have a friend at all.

The girls in my class make fun of me now, 'cause of what happened. One of them, I'm not sure which, even drew a really mean picture of what Momma probably looked like after Daddy beat her with the hammer, and slipped it into my book bag one day when I wasn't looking. And even though I never found out who did it, Jori walked into my class the next day and told them all that when he found out, even the teacher wouldn't be able to keep them safe.

He got escorted out of the school after that, and he wasn't allowed to come back in without a guardian, so he would wait for me on the sidewalk outside the school property to walk me home every day. He said that way, they would know he was serious about his words, and they wouldn't forget that he was watching them all.

It made me feel grown up, in a way, to have him there every day waiting for me. He would always smile when he saw me coming toward him; then, his eyes would narrow at each person who would look at us. Jori's always been a bit mean looking, even when he's smiling, but he's never said a coarse word to me, so I think it's just an act sometimes.

I gasp when I hear the sound of a door open

and slam violently somewhere upstairs. I can tell it's Millie because of her heavy-footed and slightly limping footsteps. She got into an accident when her and Daddy were kids; something about falling off his bike when he took a hard turn, and her foot almost got mangled because of it. She never stopped blaming him or hating him for that.

Daddy doesn't talk about it much—or Millie, for that matter—but I know he used to spend a lot of time over here, even though he would never say why.

I move off Jori's bed and make my way to the stairs. Maybe if I wait long enough, she'll head up to her room, and I can run out before she even knows I was here.

When I think I can hear her footsteps fading away, I walk as quietly as I can to the staircase and put my foot on the first step. That's when the door opens, and we see each other. She looks surprised at first, and then angry. *Very* angry.

"What are you doing in my house?" she barks at me.

"I'm sorry," I say quickly as I take a step back, wringing my hands. "I was looking for Jori, and —I'm sorry."

Millie begins to descend the stairs toward me,

and I run back to Jori's bed. It's the furthest thing away from the door, and I'm hoping I can calm her down before she gets close enough to hurt me. Everyone hurts me, and I don't know why— everyone except for Jori, anyway.

"That little son of a bitch has been in jail for the past few days," she states coolly, with a nicotine-laced cough.

"What?" I ask in shock. Her smile is about as big as my eyes are right now, and I can tell she's enjoying my dismay.

"I caught him trying to steal my car, and I called the cops. The same ones that arrested your daddy for killing your momma? They're the same ones that came and got him," she says, the smile turning cold and smug.

"But ... we have to get him out, don't we? I got money! Is that why you left him there? Oh, Millie! Please! I'll give you all my money if you get him out," I reply, a sob threatening to escape me.

She looks me up and down for a moment, before pulling a pack of cigarettes out of her bra and placing one between her yellow teeth. I wipe away my tears while she lights it and scoffs.

"You shouldn't care too much about him, you know," she says conversationally. "He's just another worthless man that this goddamn world didn't need. Just like your daddy."

I put my face in my hands and burst into tears. I don't understand why she's always so mean to Jori, why she's always so mean to me, or why she still hates Daddy over something that was clearly an accident. Millie is as bitter as the days without both of them are long, and I hate that I'm stuck here with her.

"I told your father that Doreen was fucking worthless. I tried to warn him about having kids with that bitch, and he didn't listen to me. Look at him now; sitting on death row for finally realizing he's got a pair and putting the bitch in the ground where she deserves to be. She should have taken her fucking kids with her," she mutters, before taking a long drag of her cigarette.

Millie doesn't come any closer, but she doesn't have to. Her pure hatred for me and Daddy is enough to cut me to my core, and she knows it.

I'm crying so hard by now that my body is shaking uncontrollably, and then I hear the sweetest sound I've heard in days.

"What the fuck are you doing in my room?"

I tear my hands away from my face and look past Millie. Jori's standing there with Uncle Jake beside him, looking angrier than I've ever seen him before. He pulls away from Uncle Jake's hand on his shoulder and stalks past Millie, taking me into his arms.

"Oh boy! The conquering hero is home," Millie mocks, to which Jori stiffens.

"Alright now, that's enough of that," Uncle Jake says sternly to Millie. He turns his attention to Jori and nods. "Pack some clothes so we can go."

"Should have left the little bastard in jail to rot," she remarks, taking another pull of her cigarette. "Not like he'll do any good out here, anyway."

"I said that's enough, Millie," Uncle Jake says again, giving her an angry look. "We'll be out of your hair soon. In the meantime, you need to decide if you're going to press charges against him," he says, handing her a crumpled piece of yellow paper.

Jori takes me by the hand and doesn't let go, throwing some clothes and underwear into a bag. I'm sure he'd manage better if he used both his hands, but he's keeping his promise of not leaving me alone.

Once he's got everything he needs, I help him zip the bag, which he hoists over his shoulder. As we begin to walk back toward Uncle Jake, Millie gives us both an amused glance, and Jori stops to look at her.

"You should probably *moooo*-ve before I get back. Just a friendly warning," he says, in a tone I've never quite heard him use before.

"Is that a threat, you little shit?" she asks, flicking her cigarette on his sneakers.

Jori scoffs and takes a step closer to her. "No. Just some friendly advice. Oh, and stay the fuck away from Red. I don't need you filling her head with your psychobabble bullshit."

Millie reaches for Jori's arm and yanks him away from me. He almost loses his footing and drops his bag, looking at her with utter hatred in his eyes.

"Don't you *ever* fucking touch me again! I swear to God, I'll fucking kill you if you try!" he bellows at her, clenching his fists at his side.

Millie lets him go and takes a few steps back, and even Uncle Jake looks a little shocked at Jori's reaction. She tries to keep her eyes locked with his, but she loses the battle of wits and turns, damn near tripping on her way up the stairs.

Jori leans down and picks his bag up off the floor, and with that, he reaches for my hand, giving it a tug, keeping himself between me and Uncle

Jake as we walk past him. Even though Millie is up there somewhere, hiding, Jori lets me go up the stairs first, keeping a hand on my back. When we get to the kitchen, he drops his bag to the floor and wraps his arms tightly around me.

"She can't keep us apart. None of them can. I promise," he whispers into my ear.

22

Uncle Jake's House, 1992

"Weren't you scared?" I ask him quietly. I'm sitting in the backseat of Uncle Jake's station wagon, huddled up against Jori. He runs a hand back through his hair and shakes his head. His eyes are trained on the houses going by us in a blur, and I wonder if he's lying to me, since he hasn't looked at me after getting in the car.

His arm is firmly wrapped around my shoulder, holding me close, and every now and then, I can see him steal a glance at the rear-view mirror. He's watching Uncle Jake carefully, because he knows the secret I've been keeping from everyone except him.

"How long are you staying with us?" I ask, nudging him. It's bothering me that Jori won't look at me right now—it makes me feel like he's hiding a secret in his eyes that he doesn't want me to see.

"Until after court," he replies curtly.

I sigh and try to pull away from him, but he pulls me back against his body. He still won't look at me, and I don't know when court is, so I have no idea when Uncle Jake will turn him back over to Millie, and it hurts me. I hate that he's suffering, and I hate that he lives a life thinking no one wants him around, because I do. I'd give up a thousand nights of what he thinks is a perfect life, of sleeping in a bed with two parents under the same roof, if it meant seeing Jori genuinely happy for one entire day.

A few moments later, Uncle Jake pulls his car into the driveway and turns to face us after turning it off.

"Listen, I know this isn't exactly the best scenario, and I get that things look really bleak right now, but I'll do my best to make this easy on both of you, okay? Gracie, you're still sleeping in your bedroom, and Jori, you can sleep on the couch or I can make up the guest room for you, whichever you prefer. I'll expect you to do chores around the house like Gracie does, and that'll be the cost of living under my roof. Does that sound fair?" he asks him.

"Yeah. Whatever," Jori replies, glancing at him and shrugging. "As long as we have an understanding on other matters, I'm pretty sure we'll get along just fine."

"You'd do well to remember who the adult is here, and then we'll get along just fine," Uncle Jake shoots back at him.

Jori scoffs and rolls his eyes before he reaches for his bag and shoves the door open. As soon as he's on his feet, he leans back into the car and reaches for my hand. He finally locks eyes with me and smiles when I take his hand and let him help me out of the car.

"Honey, we're home," he says in a soft, playful tone. I grin up at him as we wait for Uncle Jake to open the door from the garage to the house. Once we're inside, it's my turn to lead Jori around for a change. I take him through the kitchen and into the living room before we reach the hallway that leads to the rooms and bathrooms.

I walk him all the way to the back of the house and into the guest room. He walks in, sets his bag down, and looks around, before shrugging and turning to face me.

"I'm sorry I left. I just had some shit to take care of," he says, sucking his teeth and glancing away from me.

"It's okay," I reply, clasping my hands in front of me. "I knew you'd come back."

He cuts his eyes toward me and arches an eyebrow, a grin playing across his youthful face. With a nod, he walks over to the bed, flops down on it, and pats the extra space next to him.

"I don't know Jori," I reply with a nervous glance over my shoulder. "I don't wanna make Uncle Jake mad, 'cause who knows where he'll send you off to if he doesn't want us hugging each other so much."

Jori props himself up onto his elbows and rolls his eyes. "Red. Chill. Come here, lie down, and let's take a nap—just like we used to do in the tree house. I'm tired; I've barely slept in the past few days, and I really just want to get some sleep."

I nod. Me and Jori have never done anything wrong; not the way Uncle Jake does to me. We just like to cuddle each other 'cause it's easier for both of us to fall asleep that way.

I push the door closed, leaving it open just a crack so Uncle Jake can see we're just sleeping if he checks in on us, which I'm sure he will at some point. I walk over to the bed and kick my sandals off, before climbing on and turning my back to Jori. He puts an arm around my waist and lets out a sigh, before placing his chin on the top of my head. He's always been so damn tall and he likes to make a game of reminding me that he's bigger than me sometimes.

I don't mind it.

He never means anything in a cruel way, and I very much like being able to feel him against me while we're sleeping. That's what best friends are for—to make you feel better when the world decides to turn against you.

"We'll be having dinner in a couple of hours," Uncle Jake says, pushing the door open. I jump and try to pull away from Jori, but he tightens his grip around my waist.

"Okay," he replies with a loud, exaggerated yawn. "See ya then."

I open my eyes with a start. I sit up, rub them, and glance up at the Hello Kitty clock on the wall by my bedroom door. I hate that stupid thing, but Uncle Jake says that if we keep my room young, it'll keep me that way too, just how he likes me.

I can't shake the feeling that something's not right, but nothing seems to be standing out. With a shrug, I lie back down and turn on my side, pulling my blankets up to my chin when I hear a noise coming from the bathroom.

My eyes linger on the hallway and when I see can see the dim light has been turned on, I push the blankets off and get to my feet. It won't do me any harm to find out if something's wrong, because it's not doing me any good just to sit here and wonder. Besides, Jori's here now, and if something bad is happening, I'll run to his room and tell him. He's brave—a lot braver than any man I've ever known—with the exception of Daddy—and he'll make sure the house is safe.

I quietly make my way to my bedroom door and open it a little wider so I can peek out into the hallway. When I'm sure no one is there, I lean my head out the door and crane my neck to get a look at Uncle Jake's room, which is closed. I can hear him snoring, so I know it's not him in the bathroom I hear.

I don't know if I should run for Jori now, or if my scream will be loud enough to wake them both up if there's an intruder in the house, but I decide it's time to try and be brave like Daddy and him.

I step out of my room, flatten my back against the wall, and begin to creep toward the bathroom. The door is slightly ajar and that's why I was able to see the light in the hallway. My heart is racing the closer I get, but Daddy and Jori wouldn't turn away, so neither will I.

"Hello?" I ask when I finally reach the door and give it a nudge with my foot. When I don't get an answer, I push it open some more and raise my eyebrows when I see Jori leaning over the sink.

"Give me a minute," he says in a shaky voice, pushing the door closed.

Something's definitely not right. Jori's never closed a door in my face for as long as I've known him, and I'm not gonna let him start now.

"Hey," I say, opening the door again and stepping in. He turns his face away and I can see his arms are shaking. He's got a tight grip on either side of the sink with both of his hands, and his knuckles look damn near white with the force he's using.

"Hey," I repeat a little louder, as I walk over and place a hand on his arm. "What's going on?"

Jori sniffles and looks down at my hand on his arm. I can tell he's trying to find comfort in my touch, but his words actually shock me.

"Please don't touch me right now," he says softly.

I immediately take my hand away from his arm and try to catch his eyes in the mirror, but he won't meet them. No matter how much I shift or sigh next to them, he just won't look at me.

But there's something very familiar about the way he's behaving right now, and it's making me feel sick to my stomach.

He manages to take a deep breath before he finally raises his face to look in the mirror, careful not to meet my eyes. I watch as he runs his hands back through his hair, before opening the medicine cabinet and pulling out the half used tube of toothpaste. He reaches into the band of his gym shorts and pulls out his toothbrush.

As soon as he begins scrubbing his mouth like he's trying to knock his own teeth out, I drop to my knees and start crying softly.

I've done that so many times before.

"Oh Jori," I weep into my hands.

He spits into the sink before he reaches down a hand and places it on my head for a moment. Then, I can hear the sound of the furious scrubbing before he spits again. Once he's washed his mouth out vigorously with water, he turns off the faucet and reaches down for me.

"Don't cry," he says, pulling me up to my feet. "Red, look at me."

Jori gently pries my hands away from my face, and I can see that his eyes are as red as mine, his face is a sick shade of pale, and his mouth is trembling slightly, but the sad smile on his lips is what shatters my heart.

"If he does it to me instead, he'll leave you alone."

23

Sing Sing Correctional Facility
Present Day

"We didn't get to talk much last time you were here. How ya been?" I ask Gracie, leaning an arm on the counter and smiling across the window. I'm kind of surprised she decided to change her hair color, because that's what I always felt made my baby girl so special, but I'm sure she has her reasons, and if she feels I should know them, she'll tell me.

"That was my fault, sorry," she replies with a

laugh. "I wasn't so sure you'd see me, so it was a nice surprise when you told me to come up. But I've been doing good, Daddy. How about you?"

I nod once and return her smile, "I'm doing alright. We have our routines here and it helps the time go by, you know?"

Gracie's smile falters, but she's trying to stay upbeat for my sake. I don't want to upset her, so I lean back in my chair and use a finger to make a halo around my head and raise an eyebrow.

"Oh! I almost forgot I did this," she says with a laugh. "Do you like it? It's more Blackburn and less evil monster spawn from Hell, I think."

I close my eyes and chuckle. She did it to get rid of the Doreen in her, and it's about the same thing I would do given the circumstances, I guess.

"I think you look beautiful, baby," I reply warmly.

"Thank you," she says with a shy smile, her face blushing a pale crimson red. We sit in silence for a moment and she begins to chew her lower lip. Something's on her mind and that's her tell-tale sign—it has been since she was a little girl.

"What's on your mind?" I ask, leaning forward again and propping my elbow on the counter. I hate that my movements probably come across as robotic, but there's only so much space in this fucking room, and I can't really get comfortable no matter how hard I try.

She lowers her eyes and begins to pick at the chipped counter, and I smile. I've seen that before a few years ago, and it makes me wonder how Jori's doing these days, too. It astounds me how similar yet so fucking different these two are.

"Have they given you a … um …" Her voice trails off, and she reaches up to wipe a tear away from her face.

"No. Not yet, and I'm not worried about that, so you don't worry about it either, you understand? I'm more concerned with having some good memories for my little girl to cherish rather than the reality of everyday life," I reply sternly. "Gracie? Look at me, please. Do not worry about me, okay? I'm gonna be fine, and you should be, too."

She nods and attempts to force a smile on her face, but it looks more like a grimace and I start to laugh.

"You used to make that same face when you were a little girl. Any time I tried to scold you, you would try to smile but make *that* face and leave me in stitches. Some things never change, huh?"

Gracie laughs as she wipes away the rest of her

tears. I grin while she takes a deep breath to calm herself down, and decide to change the subject now the chance has presented itself.

"So where are you living these days? Still in Cold Spring?"

"No," she replies with a firm shake of her head. "I'm out in West Virginia; Harpers Ferry."

"Oh yeah? Do you like it out there?"

"Yeah, it's nice and quiet and no one there knows about what happened, so it's kind of a fresh start, I guess," she says.

You deserve it, I think with a smile on my face and a pain in my heart. Doreen was never good to Gracie, and the way she treated her alone would make anyone run for the hills when the opportunity presented itself.

"Hey, so let me ask you something else," I begin, pausing for a moment to switch the receiver to my other hand. "How's Jori doing? Have you seen him lately? I was always worried about that kid."

There's a new smile on Gracie's face, one that tells me she's still friends with him, but something about that isn't sitting right with me.

"Jori's fine, Daddy. He lives in Harpers Ferry too. With me," she says softly.

I clear my throat, trying to fight against the

tightening feeling inside it, and wait for her to continue.

"He's great; wonderful really. I never knew we could come so far just from being best friends, you know? But Jori's always been there for me and he still is. I love him so much."

I let my breath out in a rush, but decide not to jump to conclusions because once upon a time, I loved Millie too. That was until she turned on my boy and started treating him like a piece of trash instead of her own blood.

"Love him how?" I ask quietly.

Gracie raises her eyebrows in confusion before she lets out a giggle and says the words I knew in my heart were going to fall from her lips.

"He's my guy, Daddy," she explains in an embarrassed tone. The kind of tone all little girls who introduce their first boyfriends to their fathers use in hopes to quell the disbelief that their child is all grown up.

I feel ill; sick to my stomach, because he knew. I told him when he asked me, and he chose to continue this relationship in a way he never should have.

And with as angry as I am, with all the tears that are forcing themselves down my face, I can't find hatred in my heart for him. Jori's always been lost, and Gracie has been the only ever constant he's had, but now I'm faced with breaking her heart or letting her continue this completely fucked up relationship.

I run a hand over my face to wipe away the tears before they have a chance to even begin and take a deep breath. I look up into Gracie's eyes and sigh heavily. She looks so curious and confused at my reaction that I don't know if I have the power to do this just yet.

But as her father—as *their* father—I have to try.

"I need you to do something for me," I begin softly. "I need you to stop whatever it is you're doing with Jori."

Gracie leans back in her chair, a look of devastation on her face. What she doesn't understand is that this isn't just a father disapproving of his daughter's boyfriend; this is a father trying to save his children from each other. A father doing his best to stop a sick love that never should have come to be.

"What?" she asks, her voice becoming shrill. "Why?"

I glance up at the camera over her head. I don't know how much time we have left, but I'm going to stop this visit before I tell her things Jori should have a long time ago.

"Ask Jori."

With those words, I hang up the receiver and knock on the door. I know we have more time left in our visit, but I can't face my little girl right now, knowing what's been going on.

Hopefully, she'll forgive me and come back and see me again. If she doesn't, I'll understand and keep her tucked in my heart, and hope that one day she'll know I've only ever tried to be a good father.

To her and to Jori.

Maybe she'll forgive him one day, too.

24

Red's been exceptionally quiet since I picked her up from the prison. She doesn't even seem to want to acknowledge that I'm in the car with her, so I'm assuming she didn't have the best visit with Hoyt today.

I'm not gonna poke the bear and ask her, because she'll tell me when and if she wants to talk about it. It's not every day she shows her temper, but she's got a hell of a lot of Doreen in her, regardless of the hair color change.

I've seen it once, maybe twice, and even though

it wasn't directed at me, I made damn sure to never get on her bad side after that.

I chuckle at the memory because it's the first time I've seen her be "bad", and it was the last time, too. Her temper may rear its head once in a great while, but the way she exploded that night—it was fucking *magic.*

I don't bother reaching for her hand because the way she's sitting, I'd have to wrestle her arms apart, and I'm not in the mood for it.

The drive back to the hotel is a silent one, but once we get inside, I'll surprise her and tell her I've extended our stay by a couple of weeks so she can stay near Hoyt without having to drive back and forth so much.

As soon as I park and shut the car off, I open my door and begin walking around the front to open Red's for her, but she's already out of the car and on her way into the building.

I roll my eyes and break into a jog so I can catch up to her. She's made it to our room already and is slipping the key card into the hole, pushing it open and walking in. I follow her into the room, brows furrowed in confusion as she picks our bags off the bed we had them piled on and tosses them onto the floor.

She sits down, arms still firmly laced across her chest, and a strange stare is suddenly fixed on me. I throw my car keys onto the table and walk over to her, but as soon as I make a move to sit next to her, she raises her hands and motions for me to sit on the other bed.

"What happened today that put you in this mood?" I finally ask, staring at her intently.

Red clears her throat and looks away from me, but only for a moment, before she straightens her shoulders and replaces her stare with a glare.

"When was the last time you saw Hoyt?" she asks me bluntly.

"What?"

"Hoyt? When was the last time you saw him?" she repeats.

"Fuck if I know. Probably when the cops arrested him," I lie with a shrug. "Why? Did he tell you something different?"

Red's watching me carefully. She wants to see if my demeanor will change or if I'll potentially slip up and reveal that I'm lying to her, but when you spend your entire fucking life being lied to, you tend to pick up a few pointers.

She looks down for a moment, uncrossing her arms, then turns her face away. She's too far into trying to figure out whatever the hell it is she's hiding from me that she doesn't know how to put it into words.

That fucks with me so much. We've always been able to talk to each other, and now it seems like she doesn't know if she can. The longer it takes her to speak, the more I can feel myself starting to sweat. I hope by the time she finds her words, I'm not a soaking fucking mess riddled with the lies I've been telling her and myself for the past few years.

"We talked about you today," she begins slowly. "He asked me how you were doing and I told him that we're together. He told me to break it off and when I asked him why, he told me to ask you."

I laugh loudly.

Once—only once—and then I clear my throat. I'm so fucking relieved right now, because had he told her the truth, she would have more than likely left already.

"Sorry," I reply, wiping my sweaty palms on my shorts. "Think about this, Red. Which one of the adults hasn't lied to you or me or both of us at the same time at some point in our lives? I don't know what Hoyt's getting at with his shit, but I haven't seen him since the cops took him. Maybe he wants you two to get closer and that means taking me out of the picture, but I honestly have no fucking clue what he's talking about."

She narrows her eyes at me. She still can't decide if I'm telling her the truth either, but she knows I'm making a valid point. They all lied to us —Hoyt, Doreen, Jake, and Millie. She doesn't know the true extent of their lies like I do.

Finally, she lets out a sigh and gets to her feet. "If you knew something, you'd tell me, right?"

I look up at her, wringing her hands to the point of damn near twisting her fingers all the way around, and get to my feet.

"I'd tell you everything I can to make this life better for the both of us," I say, walking over and putting my arms around her shoulders. I rest my chin on top of her head and sigh in relief when she leans into me.

If what I know *would* make this better, I would tell her without hesitation, but it won't. it'll only further fuck with her mind, knowing there's a reason we've always been drawn to each other, and I refuse to be yet another reason Red has been let down in her life.

"Want some good news?" I ask her.

"I would love some," she replies into my chest.

"I extended our stay. Being this close to Hoyt—I can tell it puts you in a better mood, so we'll be here for another couple of weeks. Plenty of time to keep fucking up the sheets."

Red giggles and pulls back, looking up at me and I grin.

"You're alright, Jori Davidson," she says softly.

"You're not so bad yourself, kid," I reply before I lean down and give her a gentle kiss on the lips.

My mind is made up in this moment. I refuse to ruin her life any further than it already has been. I'll keep this secret from her because I know it's the only way I'll be able to keep *her*.

Uncle Jake's House, 1998

I've spent the past three hours trying to tell myself that what I'm going to do tonight is the right thing. I don't need the convincing, because he's gonna get what's coming to him. I learned to live with what the bastard did to me, but then I had the dream again.

I woke up in a cold sweat with my heart in my throat, thinking. It's always the same miserable dream—the one where I walk down the hallway of his house and find Jori scrubbing his mouth desperately to try and get rid of the sweaty, salty taste of Jake.

It didn't last longer than his stay with us in that cesspool, but it was long enough to stick out in my subconscious, where I tried to bury all the bad things that have happened to me.

I don't care if I get caught, and I sure as hell don't care what happens to me anymore, because the only person who should be cared for is the one I plan on getting a little payback for.

I haven't seen Jake in the couple of months that have passed since I turned eighteen years old. That's when Jori showed up at the door and we ran away from this fucking place. We ran far enough to where we thought we could forget everything, but every now and then, that damn dream comes back to haunt me.

The only way to stop it is to stop *him.* I hope that when this is all over, I'll never have that dream again, but only time will tell, I guess.

I still don't know if Jake will listen to me, or if we'll have it out, but I'll make damn sure he understands the reasons *why* before all is said and done.

The cell phone on the empty passenger seat next to me vibrates, and I take my hand off the wheel to reach for it. Holding it at eye level, I can see it's Jori calling me again, but I send him to voicemail for the fifth time. He knows where I'm going, but I didn't tell him why, because I didn't want to risk him getting worked up over this. He would have insisted on coming to keep the distance between me and Jake, but I'm a grown woman now, and Jake doesn't like women—he likes little girls, and on that one rare occasion, he traded pussy for dick.

I lower my window and reach for the cigarettes I hide in the visor of my car, and slide one between my lips. The anger I'm feeling right now is unrivaled to anything I've ever felt before, and I need this fucking smoke to help me regain my bearings. My words need to be cohesive and my speech I've gone over a thousand times in my head has to be spoken carefully enough that he fucking gets it.

Once the lighter pops up from the charger, I grab it and light the end of my cigarette. Replacing it, I catch a glimpse of myself in the rear-view mirror and sigh. I don't even look like myself right now. I look just like Doreen—angry, bitter, and cruel, but unlike her, the target of my rage deserves it.

I can't wake up like I did anymore.

I can't live my life knowing that the man who

put my best friend through the same hell he put me through is living some semblance of a normal life because no one is the wiser.

The sign for Cold Spring looms like an ominous warning above me, and as I drive underneath it, I take another drag from my cigarette.

All of it—every last misdeed that was done to me, to Jori—ends as soon as I get to Jake's front door.

"Answer the fucking phone!" I yell into Red's voicemail. She woke up shaking and then left in a blaze of anger and fury, and I'm so fucking worried she's gonna get herself into a mess she won't be able to recover from.

After she sent me to voicemail the second time, I got in my car and took off after her. She's got a good lead on me, but I can remember where Jake lives, and if she was telling me the truth, that's where I'll find her.

I'm driving so goddamn fast that if a cop in any state catches me, I'll get pulled over. I don't care, as long as they just ticket me and let me go. There's plenty of Hoyt's money left to pay for it anyway, and I can take care of it before she knows. She always tells me to slow down because she's afraid I'm gonna kill myself, driving the way I do, but sometimes I just like to show off for her. Besides, I never drive faster than I can deal with, and this thing was built for speed anyway.

I punch her phone number into my cell again and hold it up to my ear while I swerve around a truck and punch the gas. I have to make up the time; I need to get there when she does. Red isn't built for hurting people—she's built to *be* hurt.

I let out an angry yell when the phone just rings and rings. If she didn't cut my call off, that means she's already there, and I'm not sure how far away from Cold Spring I am right now.

Another thirty minutes of frantic missed calls later, and I cross the town line. Luckily, Jake doesn't live too far deep into this shitty little town, so I should be at his house in ten minutes tops.

I slow down considerably because the cops in this place know who I am, and ever since I got arrested for stealing Millie's piece of shit car, they've had a hard-on for me. The bitch never did press charges, and I got to stay in her house until I was old enough to leave and take Red with me. It worked out because she always made damn sure to never come down to my room when I was there, and spent most of her miserable life outside the house after that, probably off grazing in a pasture somewhere; I never fucking cared enough to ask.

I turn the car onto Jake's road and creep painfully slowly until I get to his place. Just as I had suspected, Red's car is already parked out front, which means she's inside without me.

Fuck.

I park the car, hop out, and run for the front door. I can hear a commotion inside, but not loud enough to get the attention of any neighbors—unless they were as close to the door as I am.

"Red?" I ask, pushing the unlocked door open and stepping inside. My breath catches in my throat when I see what a mess the living room is in. It's a clear sign that a scuffle of sorts took place in here, and I'm so fucking scared right now—not for me, but for my Gracie. If something happened to her because I couldn't get here fast enough, I'll never fucking forgive myself.

"Red?" I call out louder.

"I'm here," she calls back faintly.

I turn around and close the door, flipping the lock before I head toward the back of the house.

"Come on out, babe," I plead, my voice cracking. If she steps out of whatever room she's in, I'll know she's okay; if she doesn't, she's more than likely in trouble.

I can hear the shuffling sound of feet moving on the floor, and I brace myself in case it's not her. But when she finally appears in the hallway with blood on her hands and a thousand yard stare in her eyes, I rush over to her.

"Are you hurt? Did he hurt you?" I ask, grabbing her by the arms and checking her over.

"No. He'll never hurt anyone ever again," she replies bluntly. I step back as soon as I realize she's holding a knife, and slowly move to pry it from her hands.

"I should have done this sooner. Then, he never would have put his hands on you," she says, her eyes finally focusing again, and turning her head slowly toward Jake's room.

"Fuck. Red. *Fuck*," I reply through gritted teeth. I take a deep breath and kiss her firmly on the forehead, telling her to wait for me while I go in and check on Jake.

A wave of nausea washes over me. He's lying on the floor by the side of his bed, and he looks like he's been attacked by a wild fucking animal. I guess when a caged beast has been poked and prodded enough times, the results are catastrophic, but I never expected this.

"What the fuck is that?" I mumble to myself as I take a step closer. It only takes a moment to realize what I'm looking at, and I take in a deep breath, trying my best not to dry heave. "Holy shit."

"I told him I wanted to let him play with me one more time—for old time's sake, because that's the only way I knew I could get him to let his guard down," Red says in a faraway voice from the hallway. "And when he took his pants off and told me to get on my knees, I did. I reached down for his little fucking pecker and I bit the tip off; then, I used the knife to cut off what I couldn't rip away with my teeth."

I turn and I look at her. She's looking at Jake's body on the floor, and there's so much fucking blood on her arms that I didn't notice it also on her mouth.

"Okay. Okay," I say, putting my hands on my hips and pacing the room. "I'll take care of this. You go fix up the living room and I'll figure out how to get rid of this shit. I swear, no one will ever know what happened to him, but I need you to do that for me, okay? Go ahead and pick up the living room, and I'll fix this."

Red turns her eyes away from Jake and disappears stiffly down the hallway. I don't know how I'm going to cover this up, and I don't know if we're gonna get away with what happened tonight, but I'll take the blame for everything that's happened here if we're caught.

Hoyt did it for me without hesitating, and I understand now that it's because he loves me as much as I love Red, even though it's in a different way.

A lion will always lay down his life for the lamb he loves, and it's the least I can do for Red if the time ever comes.

Present Day

I'm lying on my own bed right now, and Jori's not too happy about it. He's huffing and puffing; rolling on to his back, on his side, then back the other way again. He's punched his pillow at least five times, complaining that it's "too fucking fluffy", but I know his agitation comes from me not being right next to him.

He folds an arm behind his head and turns his face to look at me—I know it, not because I'm looking at him, but because I can feel his eyes boring into me.

"Are you hungry?" he asks in a gruff tone. I have to bite my lip to keep from laughing. He's rarely ever angry with me, and if his voice is any indication of how he's truly feeling, maybe it's for the best that I don't play this little game for longer than he can actually manage it.

"No. Thank you, though," I reply quietly, turning my back to him. But as long as I've still got the spirit in me, I'll drag it on a bit longer.

"Fine," he says, moving off the bed and getting to his feet. He picks up the remote control and shuts the television off, then tosses it onto the small table between the beds. "I'm going out. See you when I see you."

"Take a key card in case I'm asleep when you get back," I advise him, yawning loudly.

"Whatever," he scoffs. I can hear him fiddling with the paper envelope before he walks out the door and slams it loudly behind him.

I wait until I can't hear his footsteps in the hallway anymore before I move off my bed and reach for his duffle bag. I can't shake the feeling Jori's hiding something from me, but I have no idea what it could possibly be.

Hoyt told me to ask him, and when I did, he completely rebuffed the idea as quickly as he could. That was enough to confirm my suspicions that he's not being entirely truthful with me, but about what?

I pull the zipper open, flip the bag over, and give it a shake until everything falls out onto my bed. I don't see anything unusual right away—clothes, socks, underwear, condoms; not that he ever uses them.

Unless ...

I feel sick to my stomach as I hold up the box. Maybe that's his secret. Maybe he's fucking someone else besides me, and somehow Hoyt found out. *Ever the doting father, even behind a thick pane of glass,* I think sadly as I drop the box on the bed and wrap my arms around myself.

I guess this is what heartbreak feels like, and it's really no one's fault but my own for being so damn nosy. I reach for the remnants of the spilled bag and begin to refill it, shoving the condoms at the bottom and covering them up as much as I can, before I put his bag back on the floor.

In a way, it doesn't make sense. We spend damn near every waking moment together. *Except for when I left to see Hoyt without telling him.*

I put my face in my hands and gently begin to sob. The only man in my life who has never let me down is the only one who's going to die any given day, while the one who dangled hopes and dreams of a better tomorrow has been getting his rocks off with someone else behind my back.

I should have known better than to put him in my heart deeper than I have my own father. A girl's first love set aside for someone who's deceived me for God only knows how long.

I angrily wipe the tears away from my face and get to my feet. I've spent about twenty minutes crying over this, and to me, that's twenty minutes too long. I reach down for my bag and carry it toward the desk the television is sitting on, and reach for the pad and pen—compliments of the hotel, of course, because he'll get nothing more from me. Not until he can prove me wrong—not until he can make me believe I'm the only girl he loves.

I take a deep breath as I begin to pen an anger-filled *Dear John* letter before I sign the letter *Gracie* and underline it at least five times. Red died a long time ago and he's never been able to let go of that young girl who always looked at him like he could capture the stars in the sky and string them up just for her.

I don't bother grabbing a key card because I have no intention of coming back. I'll find a bus depot to sleep in until I can see Hoyt again. I'll say my goodbyes to him after I ask his forgiveness for being such a fucking failure, and then I'll mourn him when he dies.

As I walk out of the room and down the hallway, I feel the carpeting under my bare feet and realize that, in my haste, I've forgotten to put my sandals on. It doesn't matter; if I'm going to sleep in a dirty terminal like a vagabond, I may as well look the part.

I push the door open to the back of the hotel and I'm greeted by an unwelcome sight. Jori's standing there with a confused smile on his face and a large pizza box in his hand.

"Going somewhere?" he asks curiously.

"Fuck off," I reply, pushing past him and walking down the sidewalk.

"Whoa! Hey! Red!" he calls out, as he begins to jog to catch up to me. Jori grabs onto my elbow tightly and attempts to spin me around to face him, but when I don't budge, he walks around to look at me. His face is a mixture of confusion, anger, and sadness, but I don't care. He can save it for whatever whore he's fucking.

"My name is Gracie. *Gracie;* why is it so hard for you to call me that?" I shout at him, tears threatening to spill again.

"Okay, okay. Calm down," he says, leaning down and placing the pizza box on the ground. "I'm sorry, Gracie. What's the problem?"

"Let go of me. I'm done playing your games. I know your fucking secret and I'm not going to do this anymore!" I shout, trying to pull my arm out of his grip.

Jori arches his eyebrows and his mouth hangs open slightly. He reaches for my other arm and his hands become like vises on me as he leans forward, a pleading look in his eyes.

"That shouldn't change the way you feel about me, Gracie. It shouldn't—it didn't change the way I feel about you when I found out," he says in a rush, his lower lip trembling. "I love you! Please? Please tell me you still love me. No one has to know."

I narrow my eyes at him and try to pull away again, but Jori pulls me against him as his body becomes wracked with tears.

"No! No; you're not leaving me. Not over this. I

swear to god. Not over something as fucking stupid as this," he sobs into my hair.

"How long did you think you could hide this from me, you piece of shit?" I ask, angrily shoving him away.

He looks at me and raises one hand in the air before dropping it again. "It's my fault for not telling you, and I know that's what Hoyt wanted you to know, but … I know we can get past it; we're stronger than this, Gracie. What we have is so much stronger than blood."

I shake my head and cross my arms over my chest. Why he thinks I can forgive a betrayal like this is beyond me, but the way he looks right now —the sadness, the pleading—I've never seen him like it before, and it's breaking my heart all over again.

"Our relationship is *ours,* no one else's; fuck what people think. Hell, if everyone in our lives were so great, they would have told us. I had to find out the truth by coming up to see Hoyt and asking him," he continues, bitterly wiping away his tears.

"What?" I ask in confusion. "You came to see Hoyt?"

"Well, when you find something like a fucking

birth certificate with your name on it, you kind of wanna ask the person's name who fucking made you if it's true," he says, taking a shaky breath.

I blink rapidly a few times and stare at Jori. I'm not entirely sure what he just rambled, but if it's what I think it is, that means—*oh my god.*

"You're my brother?" I ask him, my voice trembling.

The look on Jori's face tells me he realizes that what he thought I was going crazy about wasn't the issue. It was something completely different, and he just inadvertently let the secret he's been keeping from me out into the open.

"Fuck," he says, dropping his head and putting his face in his hands.

I drop my bag and sit on the sidewalk, pulling my knees to my chest and wrapping my arms around them. I take a deep breath and hold it for a moment as Jori sits down on the pavement next to me.

"Want some pizza?" he asks lamely.

I nod, even though I'm not hungry, and he leans back to retrieve the box. He flips the top open, holds it out to me, and I reach for one of the large slices, nibbling the tip of it thoughtfully.

"Why do you have condoms in your bag?" I ask, glancing at him.

"You went through my bag?" Jori asks, wiping away the rest of his tears.

I nod and take another nibble of the pizza, my eyes lingering on him. "I had a feeling you were keeping something from me and I went through your shit. I found the condoms and thought you were seeing someone behind my back."

He balances the box on his lap as he takes a huge bite of his slice and shakes his head. Jori holds up a finger while he chews as quickly as he can, then looks at me.

"I don't know why I have them. Never bought them before, and I guess I just decided to when I saw them. Maybe change things up one night, you know? But I'm not seeing or fucking anyone else. Or anyone now, probably, for that matter," he says glumly, dropping his slice back into the box.

"Don't be gross," I say, making a face and reaching for his slice. I hand it back to him and continue to nibble on mine, leaning my head against his shoulder.

This should change things—a lot of things. And maybe it's the shock of him thinking I didn't know, which I didn't for sure, but I kind of knew there had to be something more to the connection I feel with him. I just didn't expect it to be *this.*

I let out a sigh and look up at the evening sky. It'll be dark soon, and I'll have to decide if I want to sleep in my own bed tonight.

"Can I ask you something?"

"Yeah," he replies quietly.

"What did Hoyt say? Like, what was his reasoning behind all of it?"

Jori cuts his eyes away from me and focuses his attention on the cars driving by on the street, and shrugs.

So there's another secret.

"Um, he said they gave me to Millie 'cause Doreen didn't want to have kids. Then, they had you, and he wanted to be able to raise one of us, so they kept you."

I sigh and pull away from his arm. "I'm sorry."

"Nah, don't be. We still grew up together without knowing it, you know? So that's kind of rad, if you think about it. I just never thought it would ever … " His voice trails off as he steals a glance at me. "So what now?"

I can hear the nervousness in his voice, but most of all I can hear the longing, the needing, and the wanting.

"I don't know," I reply honestly. "Knowing what I know now *should* make me feel different, but the fucked up thing is that I'm just relieved that you're not cheating on me. Pretty lame, huh?"

Jori shrugs as he closes the pizza box and sets it on the other side of him. I look at him carefully and shake my head when I see his lower lip trembling again.

"Why do we have different last names, then?" I ask suddenly.

"Doreen Davidson," he replies glumly.

I sigh loudly. Even in death, that bitch is still trying to ruin my life, and if I let her do it again, she wins. But this is so wrong it can never be right —can it?

"I'll make a deal with you," I say, turning my body to face him.

Jori glances down at me and arches an eyebrow. I can usually see so much in his eyes, but right now they look so dead and void that I don't know what the right or wrong thing to say is at the moment.

"If we can get Hoyt to agree to this, I'll seriously consider maintaining what we have."

He scoffs and gets to his feet angrily. "Then we may as well call it quits now, Gracie. You wanna know what he said to me when I saw him? The very last thing he said to me? 'I can forgive you for what happened before, because you didn't know, but I cannot and will not forgive you for what you do after you leave this room.' And since those are your terms and I already have your answer, I guess this is over."

"Wait a sec," I say, getting to my feet. "Let *me* talk to him about it. You're not exactly tactful when you want something. Trust me, I know this from experience," I say with a smirk.

Jori shakes his head as he reaches down for the pizza box. "If you're hinging your hopes on Hoyt giving us his blessing, there's nothing left here and it's so fucked up. I don't understand why I can never find someone who loves me as much as I love them. Even when I found out, I went to the man with hopes of maybe forming some kind of bond with him, and you were all he was concerned about, and that hurt me so much. I love you, Gracie, but that hurt, to be brushed off again."

He turns on his heel and begins to walk toward the back doors of the hotel, and my face flushes hot with anger.

"Jori Davidson, don't you dare walk away from me," I warn through gritted teeth.

He shakes his head as he stops, but keeps his back to me. I know better than to try to turn him to face me—he's too angry right now, too confused at all the emotions flowing through him. So instead, I walk over and wrap my arms around him from behind, resting my cheek on his back. Jori stiffens but doesn't make a move to pull away from me.

"I always wanted a brother," I begin slowly. "I always thought that if I had one, I wouldn't have been through everything I had with Jake. I thought a brother could protect me from all the bad shit that happened to me, but I never thought the brother I wanted was suffering so much, too." Jori hiccups and I can feel a tear land on my forearm. "But I've killed for you—something I never would have thought in a million years I would be capable of doing. Do you know what that's like? And I did it because I was so tired of knowing you had been hurt for me. You willingly traded my place in Jake's fucking bed when you could have turned a blind eye and pretended things weren't the way they were. I'll never find someone who knows the shit we've been through—together and apart—and I don't want to try, either."

"What are you saying, Gracie?" he asks in a shaky voice.

"Well," I say, letting go of him and walking around to face him. I reach up and place a hand on either side of his face. "I'm saying this is gonna take some getting used to, and maybe I can forget what I know now, but what I can't forget is how much you love me and the things you've done to protect me. I still love you, Jori. I always will. I just want you to tell me that's the only thing you're hiding from me, and I'll try to be okay with this."

Jori's lip trembles as he looks into my eyes. I can see a small sliver of light returning to his, and when he nods, I let out a sigh of relief. No more secrets—everything is out in the open, and the only people who would know are already dead, will die, or have no place in our lives anymore. As long as we stay far away from this fucking place after Hoyt dies, we'll be able to live our lives how we choose to.

And for this moment, we choose to be together.

Buffalo, NY 1994

"Are you fucking crazy?" I shout at her as I hold her tightly. I have my arms firmly wrapped around Red and she's sobbing uncontrollably against my chest. I almost lost her just now because of her own mind becoming wrought with thoughts of things that have never happened.

Once she calms down—once I'm able to explain to her that *nothing* has ever happened with Ashley —I'll take her back to the cheap hotel we're staying in and rock her to sleep in my arms. Then tomorrow, I'll figure out how to get her another meerkat. She'll be so fucking upset when she realizes she's thrown it away for nothing, and I don't want that for Red. I don't ever want her to be upset over me; not if I can fucking help it.

"Leave me alone," she wails into my chest, trying to push me away, but I won't let go. I'll never let go of her, and she knows it. No matter how much she hates me right now, no matter how much she thinks I did her wrong, I'll never fucking let her go.

"I need you to calm down," I plead with her as I tighten my grip around her small, frail body. "I need you to listen to me."

Red struggles against me, and the more she does, the more I wonder how someone so small can be so damn strong.

"Nothing happened. Ever. With anyone. I would *never* do that to you, Gracie."

She gasps slightly and turns her tear-stained face up toward me. I know it's because I called her Gracie, which I rarely ever do unless it's a serious circumstance, but it can't possibly get any more serious than letting the girl I'm falling in love with know that no one else besides her has even a shot at my heart.

"Then why'd I see you guys whispering so close all the time?" she asks me uncertainly. "It bothered me every time, but I never said anything 'cause you're not mine."

I move my arms from around her waist and take her face in my hands. My heart is racing right now, and I don't think I've ever felt this rush before. Maybe this is what *being* in love is like, not just *falling*.

"I am yours, Red," I tell her, searching her sad eyes. "I've never been anyone else's, and I don't want to be. That kiss ..." My voice trails off as I shake my head. "That was the most amazing thing that's ever happened to me, and I'm sorry it doesn't seem enough to tell you how I feel about you, but I've never kissed a girl before. I'll do better next time, okay?"

Red bites her lower lip and looks down for a moment, but I gently turn her face back toward mine. I want to kiss her again—hell, I *need* to kiss her again, but I won't force it on her. If she doesn't love me the way I love her, I'll accept it and do my best to make sure that she's happy as her friend—no matter how much it'll kill me on the inside.

I'm used to it, though.

Nothing I've ever loved on this entire fucking planet has ever loved me back. There have been beautiful, rainy days that I've felt so happy on, and then the sun would shine out of nowhere, just to spite me. It would just hurt more with Red.

She kills the pain I feel every day of my useless life, and I need her in it—however she chooses to be.

"So, you believe me, right?" I ask her desperately. "I only ever went near that skank to tell her to leave you alone. I hated being around her, but I hated seeing you sad even more, so I did what I had to do to make sure you'd be happy. That's all I ever worry about, Gracie—you being happy."

She sighs as she wipes the tears away from her face, and rests her head against my chest. The shock of her almost running into traffic is wearing off, and cold, hard anger is starting to replace it. I can't let it surface because if I get angry, I'll make her cry, and I just promised her the exact opposite of that.

"I threw away my stuffy," she says sadly. "I'm sorry."

"Oh please," I reply with a huff and a shrug. "So

what? Tomorrow we can go back and I'll get you a better one."

She nods and rests a hand on my chest next to her lips. I want so much with Red. I want everything we didn't have growing up. I want everything Doreen did to her to be nothing more than a distant fucking nightmare, and I want Jake to pay for ever laying his grotty hands on her and stealing her innocence. That's the one thing that's been taken from her that I can't give her back, no matter how hard I try—but I can do my best to help her get past it if she lets me.

"It's settled then, right? Tomorrow, you'll get a brand new stuffy you can pick out, and you'll stop thinking shit that isn't real and never was," I say to her hopefully.

Red sniffles and pulls away from me. She gets to her feet, helping me up with her, and looks into my eyes silently. I'm holding my breath, and I'm afraid I'm going to turn blue and fall the fuck over before she finally answers me.

"Okay," she says softly. "I'm sorry I got so mad."

"I forgive you," I reply immediately. "And I'm sorry I didn't squash that shit earlier. If I had, you wouldn't have spent all this time thinking that."

She smiles sadly and turns her face away for a

moment, before glancing up at me again, and moving up to her tiptoes. Red puts her hands against my chest to balance herself, and as I wrap my arms around her, I feel like shit finally makes sense in this goddamn world. But when I kiss her, when I feel those soft lips pressed against mine … I finally know that it does.

Present Day

The sun peeking through the blinds in the window causes me to groan and shield my eyes. I thought I had pulled those things together tightly enough last night, but apparently I have a knack for failing at the simplest of tasks. I shift my body slightly to work out any kinks that may be left behind from sleeping, and crack an eye open.

Fuck.

Red's still fast asleep on the other bed, and it completely shits all over my mood for the day. Last night, after we had our little discussion about how things really are, we came back in and ate some more pizza before we fell asleep together in each other's arms. And yet here I am, in a bed all alone, with the other half of my heart contently sleeping so far away from me.

I roll onto my back and sigh. I don't get it—she seemed just fine with everything last night, but I wake up to find her on her own. Maybe I was moving around too much, or maybe I was snoring too loudly; either way, I hate that I can't touch her right now.

Closing my eyes, I rub my face. On the other bed, Red lets out a whimper and I raise my eyebrows as I prop myself up on my elbows to glance at her. Her body is shaking so violently now underneath the blankets that I can see it from here.

I blink a couple of times before I shove myself off the bed and go sit next to her. I use a hand to push her hair out of her face, and she lets out a gasp. She sounds like a wounded animal right now, and something is obviously plaguing her in her sleep to the point of distress.

"Babe?" I ask gently, giving her a shake. Her legs straighten in one sudden jerk, and I can see her face crumpling in her sleep. "Gracie. Come on, wake up."

Red turns onto her back, her eyes still tightly closed, and her mouth drops into the most heart-breaking frown I've ever seen in my entire life.

"Gracie," I say louder, giving her a slightly rougher shake. "Wake up."

Her chest is rising and lowering at a quickened pace, and I'm so worried she's going to have a heart attack right now that I do the only thing I can think of.

I grab her by the shoulders, sit her up, and shake her until she finally opens her eyes and looks at me in drowsy confusion.

"What?" she asks in shock. It's the feeling of being woken up so abruptly that has her stunned, but I couldn't stand to watch her reacting like that anymore.

"That's some dream you were having there, kid," I say to her softly, running a hand over her hair.

"Fuck," she mutters unhappily. She pushes my hands away from her and lies back down unhappily. "I was hoping that wouldn't happen again so soon."

I grunt and fold my arms over my chest. Part of

my newfound discomfort is that she pushed me away, and the other part is that I know all too well what her nightmare was about.

"Sorry," she says, sighing and running her hands over her face. "I know you hate it as much as I do."

"Yeah," I reply, clearing my throat. I suck my teeth and glance down at her, eyebrow arched, trying my damnedest not to look angry right now. What happened all those years ago—what I went through to give her a few weeks of peace—was worth every painful thrust and demeaning moment spent down on my knees.

And I would do it again in a heartbeat, if that's what she would need to survive this cruel world.

Red looks up at me as she shimmies over on the bed, then rubs the spot next to her. I shake my head and chuckle; she blows hot and cold so quickly, it'll end up giving me whiplash one day. I don't hesitate in lying down next to her; I'm just not sure what she wants right now, so I fold my hands over my chest and clasp them together until she turns her body toward me and waits.

I pull my hands apart and put one arm around her, bringing her closer to me, as she rests her head against my body and a hand on my stomach.

Red doesn't know what she wants, and that's okay. If I were her, I wouldn't know what to think anymore either, and the reality of that is a bit fucking hard to deal with. I know what I want with her—I want what we've always had, but she's just come to find out something that could damage most lives, and she's trying to find a way to make it work.

"I've got some shit I need to take care of today. Think you'll be alright while I'm gone?" I ask her, nuzzling the top of her head.

Red nods but offers no words. I think she deserves some time to herself, and as much as I hate being away from her, I know that giving her space will only bring her closer to me.

"Just stay a little longer?" she asks softly.

I squeeze her arm to let her know I'm not going anywhere until she tells me to. Yeah; I've got something to take care of today. Something that I should have taken care of years ago, but my main priority will always be Red's happiness, and if that means losing time right now, then so be it.

Besides, some things are definitely worth waiting for, and the last person soon to be standing is the only one left who could fuck up our lives. I refuse to let that happen.

30

Cold Spring, NY

I'm tapping the steering wheel of my car as I watch for signs of life inside of the house. I took Red for breakfast before I dropped her back off at the hotel and took off. It's best she didn't know where I was going or what I was going to do, because she's dealing with enough shit right now.

I'm quietly singing along to the song on the alt-rock station, narrowing my eyes every so often, when I think I see what I'm waiting for. But until I see the car pull into the driveway, I won't be one hundred percent sure.

"Come on, you fucking cow. Where are you?" I mutter to myself as I continue tapping along to the music.

I sigh and lean back in my seat, a hand to my forehead. Millie doesn't have any fucking friends that I know of, so where the hell is she?

I cut my eyes toward the time on the dashboard and realize I haven't been sitting here for more than half an hour, but when you're waiting to confront an evil that's ruled your life with an iron fist, time always seems to go much slower than it should.

My body slides down a bit as reach for my cell phone. I tap the screen a couple of times to bring it to life, and dial Red's number.

The phone rings at least seven times before she answers in a groggy voice. "Hello?"

"Hey baby," I greet her warmly. "Did I wake you up?"

She smacks her lips a couple of times and sighs. "No. Almost, but not quite."

"I was just calling to see how you were doing," I say as I begin to bite my fingernail. An old fucking habit that comes with nerves—pick them or bite them; it's the only way I can usually calm down when I'm pissed off or stressed out. I'm not either right now, but aggravation usually sets me on the cusp of both.

"I'm fine," she replies with a yawn. "Just tired, I guess. Hey, where did you go off to, anyway?"

I chuckle and sit back up in my chair, watching the quiet house and damn near vacant street.

"Nowhere special. I'll be back soon, I hope," I say, spitting a bit of nail out the window. "You missing me yet?"

Red giggles softly but doesn't reply any further. This fucking sucks so much, not knowing how she truly feels, but if I want to be with her, I can't force it. Either she'll come around, or she'll leave—it's not my choice anymore.

I let out a heavy sigh. "Alright. I'll let you get back to sleep. See you soon, okay?"

"Okay," she replies, disconnecting the call. I pull the phone away from my ear and stare at it. I feel like I've just been sucker-punched in the fucking heart because she didn't tell me she loved me like she always used to do when we hung up.

I throw the phone angrily in the empty seat next to me before I rub my face irritably. Maybe I'm reading too much into it, but for fuck's sake,

Red has never been this damn hard to understand before, and we've been through some pretty crazy shit.

I clear my throat and turn the key in the ignition. I'm not in the right frame of mind to sit here much longer, and I'm hoping that maybe wandering around the city for a while will help me clear my head.

I check the rear-view, then the side-view, and before I have the chance to pull out the spot I'm parked in, I see what I've been waiting for this entire time: an old beat up Jeep Cherokee that's almost older than I am, coming up the street. It amazes me that the fucking thing still runs, let alone supports Millie's fat ass.

But now I'm faced with a choice—do I stay and talk to her as calmly as I can with the hopes of not freaking out on her, or do I leave until I know I'll be able to hold a conversation like an adult?

"Fuck it," I mutter as she pulls her car into her driveway. I turn my car back off and wait until she grabs her bags of what I'm assuming are groceries, and meanders through her front door.

I push my car door open and jog quickly across the street. I couldn't give two shits if anyone sees me, but with as dead as this street has always been, it'll be a miracle if anyone does.

Once I make it to her front door, I pause to take a few steadying breaths before I raise my hand and knock.

"Just a minute!" she calls out in her nicotine riddled voice. I shudder thinking about how much worse her tone has gotten since childhood. It grossed me out when I saw her recently, and it's just as disgusting now.

I shove a hand in my pocket and glance over my shoulder. The street is still silent; no cars, no people ... no witnesses.

"What the fuck do you want?"

I turn my attention back to the now open door and the bitch who's barked such a loving greeting toward me.

"To talk," I reply evenly.

"I've got nothing to say to you. Get the fuck off my property," she says with a sneer as she attempts to close the door. I put my hand up and use my strength to push it back open.

"Good. Then you can just listen for once in your miserable fucking life," I say to her, walking in and locking the door behind me.

"And if I call the cops?" she asks, crossing her

arms over her sagging chest.

"They won't get here fast enough," I promise her with a sinister smile creeping across my lips. Millie takes a nervous step back, eyeing me warily. She told me once when I was a kid that she's always hated my smile because it reminded her of a rancid devil ready to consume the first soul it sees. I took it as a compliment and she slapped me across the face for it.

"Gracie. Hoyt. Me. We're all dead to you, do you understand me?" I state, holding up a warning finger. "You don't know us, and we don't know you. Stay the fuck out of our lives and maybe, just maybe, if you stay on your side of the fucking pasture, this will be the last time you ever have to see me again."

Millie rolls her eyes as she walks over to her rocking chair and sits down. She eyes me up and down for a moment, before she retrieves a half-smoked pack of cigarettes from her bra, slides one between her weathered lips, and lights it with the book of matches sat on the table next to her.

"You think too highly of yourself, Jori. What's to say I even think about you?" she asks with a ruptured laugh.

I tilt my head to the side and stare at her with

so much hatred it takes me a moment to compose my words. "You can stop trying to be a bad ass now, Millie. I know you're afraid of me, and you have *every* reason to believe I will do you harm if you don't take care to fuck off out of our lives."

She takes a hard, loud drag on her cigarette before she inspects her nails and shrugs. Her facade has always been nothing more than a pitiful display of courage I know she's never had when it comes to me. She's been terrified of me ever since I caught her cornering Red in my room downstairs, and even when I came by recently, she looked about ready to piss her pants. But because she thinks this is good-bye, she's trying to be a big girl now and attempt to show me who's got the bigger dick.

"Don't you worry about me. This family has always been fucking worthless, as far as I'm concerned. The only one who ever amounted to anything is my brother, and he's in jail right now over something I'm damn sure he didn't do," she says quietly, rocking slowly in her chair.

"What?"

A knowing smile starts to crease the corners of her mouth, and my heart is beginning to pound erratically in my chest. Does Millie know? And if she does, for how long? Why hasn't she turned me in?

"Hoyt never raised a hand to Doreen, no matter how mad she used to make him. He was always worried she'd take Gracie and run if he did. You had something to do with it, didn't you?" she asks with a smirk.

"Go fuck yourself," I manage to say as I turn and head for the door. As soon as my hand touches the doorknob, she issues an idle threat that turns my blood cold.

"Hey, Jori? Did you think if the cops found out, you'd be tried as an adult or a kid? I mean, you were only twelve at the time, after all."

Letting go of the knob, I turn slowly to face her, my mouth hanging slightly open, the sound of my heart beating so loudly inside my ears, I'm afraid my eardrums will burst soon.

I don't have any more words for Millie, only actions. With a shout, I lunge at her and put my hands around her throat, cutting off the scream she had attempted.

"I fucking hate you!" I scream at her through gritted teeth. Her eyes are becoming wider, her face is turning red, and my hands only become tighter as the seconds go by. But this is much too easy, much too merciful for someone like Millie Blackburn.

I move my hands quickly from around her throat to her hair and the rage helps me lift her off the chair and toss her onto the wood floors.

"You're not going to ruin our lives," I tell her as I raise my foot and bring it down across her throat. And then I do it again. And again, and again, until I've damn near decapitated her with my rage. My body is trembling, my mind isn't quite right, but I did it. I slayed the last fucking dragon that could have destroyed my life with Red.

I drop onto the couch next to her mangled body and reach for her pack of cigarettes. As calmly as I can, I pull one out and place it between my teeth, lighting it and inhaling deeply. My hands are still shaking but that'll subside soon. Getting rid of her body and any trace that I was here won't be hard. I've done it before with Ashley, and she's never been found. That was a necessity, like Millie, because she found out too, and that can't fucking happen.

I take another drag on the cigarette and chuckle quietly.

After Hoyt dies, there won't be anyone left who can keep us apart.

31

Sing Sing Correctional Facility
Present Day

"Hey, Davis. Can I ask you something?" I say to the guard as he's passing by my cell. He stops and nods, adjusting his pants at the waist, then crossing his arms over his chest.

"'Course you can, Blackburn," he replies in a friendly tone.

I walk over to my bars and drape my hands through the spaces, looking at him for a moment. I don't know how to ask him what I want to without sounding like a goddamn lunatic, but it's just something I have to know.

"How long have you been a C.O.?" I start carefully.

"Oh wow. Um, thirty years or so?" he says, scratching his head. "Yeah; about thirty. Been here for the past twenty."

"So you know a lot about the law, right?" I continue.

"I would like to think so," he replies with a chuckle.

I turn my face away for a moment, rubbing my chin before I look at him again. The friendly look on his face is giving way to curiosity because he can see the distress in my posture.

"What's on your mind, Hoyt?" he presses curiously.

"So say, hypothetically speaking, that a kid commits a crime. Would they get the death penalty? Or would they go to jail for the rest of their lives or until they're twenty-one? How does that work?" I ask him nervously.

"Well, that depends on the crime," he replies. "The harsher the crime, the harsher the punishment."

"But ... what if they felt like they didn't have a

choice? What if they're not right in the head? Is it the same thing?" I ask, feeling ill. Not once in my entire life have I ever thought of pointing the finger at my son, but if he's doing what I think he's doing with his sister, I've gotta get out of here and get them both help.

"If the perpetrator has a mental defect—which, by the way, would be up to the court to decide— then that would be something that's taken into consideration. They would more than likely end up in a psych hospital rather than jail," he explains, scratching his head.

I sigh heavily and drop my chin to my chest. I can't do that to him—I can't throw him into a place where God only knows if he would get the help he needs, when he seems to be functioning for the most part because of Gracie.

"Alright, man. Thanks," I say quietly, moving away from the bars and lying back down on my cot.

"Hoyt. What's going on?" Davis asks in confusion.

I take a deep breath and let it out in a long huff. "Nothing, man. Just some shit I've always wondered, I guess."

I close my eyes when I hear Davis' keys jingle,

followed by the sound of my bars opening. He walks into my cell and leans against the wall across from me.

"If you don't belong here, you need to tell me so I can try to help you," he says quietly. "Nothing right about sending a good man to a death he doesn't deserve."

I open my eyes, turn my face toward him, and smile. "I killed my wife. I deserve what's coming to me."

That's the first time in a very long time that I've said those words. I confessed to killing Doreen when I was on the phone with the cops. I made sure Jori was far away from the house when I called them, because he was wound so tightly I didn't want him to try and take credit for it. And he wouldn't have done it to be a big man; he would have done it because he would revel in knowing that the cops would be "afraid" of him.

"Right," Davis says, completely unconvinced of my guilt now. And to think it only took a few simple questions to get someone to finally understand. "Well, if you change your mind about that, you need to let me know. Once a date is set, there's nothing I can do for you."

I laugh and swing my legs over the side of the bed, sit up, and look him square in the eye.

"About that. Can you do me a favor, man? After I see my kid again, can you see if you can put a rush on that? I'm tired of waiting around and I would very much like this shit to be over with sooner rather than later."

Davis sighs and shoves his hands deep into his pockets. He turns his eyes toward the open cell door and nods at Morgan as he walks by. He waits until the footsteps recede down the hall and the door opens and closes shut before he looks back at me.

"I'll see what I can do."

We exchange a nod and I lie back down. Maybe if I can't save my kids from themselves, the better thing to do would be to die knowing that I tried my best to save one of them, even though I loved them both equally.

I just never got the chance to show Jori how much he meant to me, I think sadly as I close my eyes and pray for a peaceful slumber.

Harpers Ferry, WV 1998

I can't believe I killed Uncle Jake.

I've been frantic ever since I realized what I've done, and Jori still not being home isn't helping me my nerves any. I've picked up the phone at least twenty times to call the cops and turn myself in, but I keep hanging it up because I want to at least be able to say good-bye to him.

Maybe they'll put me in a cell next to Hoyt and we can catch up on the years we've missed; maybe they'll send me somewhere I can never be near him again.

Oh god, what have I done?

Part of me is terrified; a coward afraid of the things she's capable of when pushed to protect the ones she loves. A part of me is secretly proud to know what I've done—a part of Jori's life can be restored to him. He'll know a bit of normalcy because the bastard who put his hands on him will never do it again—not that he would have tried to, since we're both older now, but how many countless other children have I potentially saved?

Did he have new favorites, or was it just Jori and me that made his severed dick hard when he thought of touching and rubbing himself all over us? *It should never have been Jori; never.*

I stop pacing and go to the window in the living room again, pull the curtain aside slightly, and sigh. Still no sign of Jori, and I'm so scared he's been arrested. Would he tell them I did what he'd be accused of? Would he sacrifice himself for me yet again? I won't let them keep him if they have him; I'll tell them exactly what I did, and I'll tell them how many times I tried to chew Jake's dick off before I finally decided to cut it from his fucking body. Jori wouldn't know those things, so they can't hold him if his statement doesn't match the injuries.

With a sigh, I wring my hands and walk back to the kitchen and pick the phone up again. I stare at it for a moment as tears stream down my face, and I begin to dial the phone number for the local police station.

"Babe?"

"What?"

I let out a sound reminiscent of a squeak, and slam the phone back down into the receiver. It bounces away from the wall and hits the floor, but I don't care. I turn and run for the living room to see Jori taking off his leather jacket. He tosses it onto the couch just as I reach him, and as I wrap my arms around him, I begin to weep like small child.

"Hey," he says softly with a chuckle as he holds me close. "What's with the tears?"

"I thought something happened to you," I manage to choke out between sobs.

Jori pulls back and takes my face in his hands, smiling down into my eyes. He leans down and kisses me gently on the lips before pulling back and making a face, wiping his mouth with the back of his hand.

I can't help but laugh.

I get it; my face is a slobbering mess right now, and more than likely not exactly kissing material, but he's with me again, so I don't give a shit.

"You worry too much," he says with a half grin. "Have faith in me, kid. You know I'd never let anything happen to you."

His candor is meant to make me feel better, but another sob escapes me, causing Jori to roll his eyes and laugh. He puts his hands on my shoulders, spins me around, and leads me back toward the bedroom. Once inside, he reaches down and picks me up in his arms, kisses me again, then lays me down on the bed.

"You need to go to sleep, Red. Everything's taken care of, and if you want, we can talk about it tomorrow. I'm gonna hop in the shower, then I'll come back to bed. I expect you to be asleep when I get here, alright?" he says as he gently runs a hand over my head. That's his way of calming me down; it always has been. Gentle words and an even gentler touch punctuated with the softest, sincerest smile he can muster.

I love him for it. I always have, and I always will. Where Hoyt has been absent in my life, where Uncle Jake has failed as a father figure of sorts, Jori has always stepped in to help things make sense again.

He isn't perfect, and sometimes he fucks up along the way, but who doesn't? I roll to my side and reach for the box of Kleenex on the night-stand, and take a few tissues out to clean my face up. Jori smiles before he turns around and walks over to the dresser to pick out some fresh under-wear and gym shorts to sleep in.

I toss the used tissues into the trashcan under the nightstand and settle onto my back. It's going to take me a while to fall asleep, and I probably can't meet his timeline requirement, but I'll try my best.

"Hey," he says, lingering in the open doorway. I turn on my side to face him and pull the blankets up to my chin and offer the best smile I can under the circumstances.

"I'm serious about what I said. I took care of things so you don't need to worry, alright?"

I nod and wipe away the last of my tears as Jori grins again and disappears from sight. It isn't until I hear him turn the water on that I finally start to feel better. Even though he's held me, picked me up in his arms, and kissed me, it didn't seem real that he was here yet until I heard that sound. I don't know why, and maybe somewhere deep inside me it makes sense. It's that place where everything he does makes the world it's okay again. Maybe one day, I'll understand it more than I understand it now, but I'm afraid that when I do find that nirvana, it may hold more bad than good.

But we've always been able to withstand any storm that's come our way, and whatever that place may reveal to me, I know we'll be able to hold our ground against that, too.

By the time Jori is done in the shower and climbs into bed, I'm half asleep and much calmer than I was without him here. When he turns on his side and slides an arm around my waist, kissing me gently on the side of the head, I'm content.

I guess being a killer isn't as stressful as I thought it was when you're in the arms of another one. Some secrets can be kept, while others have been witnessed by silent and damaged innocence. The true testament of the heart is how long it's willing to hold on to such a secret to salvage what they can of the person it beats for so fiercely.

33

Ossining, NY
Present Day

Red's asleep by the time I get back to the room, which I would have expected considering it's almost one in the morning. I spent most of the day at Millie's cleaning up, after I rolled her into an old carpet I found downstairs. My original plan was to just do what I did to Jake—cut her into as many pieces as I could, then weight a duffle bag and toss her into an open body of water.

But because I don't want to field any more

questions of suspected infidelity, I left her in the trunk of the car and just came back. I have a day or two before she starts to fucking smell, so I'll be sure to get rid of her before then—somehow.

The difference between Millie and Jake is that I lit his shit up like the fourth of July and took off. As a kid, I was always interested in how things worked, so it was easy enough to make it look like an electrical malfunction was responsible for the blaze.

That's the *difference*, however; the *problem* is that my hands haven't stopped shaking. I think I'm more amped up about what I did to her because she's had it coming for fucking years, and I can only hope to God that it hurt her as much as her words had always hurt Red.

I would have done the same thing to Jake, had Red not beat me to it, I think as I pull my shirt off and toss it into the bathroom. I walk over to the bed she's lying in, and lean down to kiss the top of her head. She's in my bed tonight, and I'm hoping that means she wants me in it too, but I'll know for sure when I wake up in the morning.

With a sigh, I walk over to my bag and open it up, grab a pair of boxers, and head to the bathroom. I don't plan on taking a shower, because I don't want to wake her up, but I'll wash up as quietly as I can before I get into bed with her.

I shake my head as I close the door and hit the light switch. I look into the mirror, staring into my tired eyes, and wonder how this all went to shit so quickly.

Had I never gone to see Hoyt—had I never found that fucking birth certificate, none of this would have mattered. I doubt anyone would be dead, and we'd be peaceful and happy back in West Virginia, without Red having to question being with me now.

Does it make a difference knowing? Not to me, but to her I think it does. As I turn the knobs so a small stream of water pours out, I think about how desperately my heart beats for Red. I think about how not too long ago, her heart did the same for me. She tells me she wants to be with me, though I don't feel like she does—not anymore—and it should be okay, but it's not.

I hold the hand towel under the water before I begin to rub it over my arms. There's a tattoo I have near my elbow that made her blush the day I showed it to her. It seemed so simple at the time; nothing more than a simple outline of an animal in red ink, her favorite animal, and the word RED tattooed underneath it. She thought it was the greatest goddamn thing anyone had ever done for her, and now I'm left wondering if it holds any meaning. Does she even remember it's there?

Does it fucking matter? I wonder glumly as I move to my other arm and clean up some more. Once I'm satisfied I don't smell like cigarettes and sweat anymore, I pull my underwear off and begin to scrub my legs before I wet the towel again and clean up my dick, then put on the clean boxers. I toss the hand towel on top of my sweaty underwear and kick them under the sink. I'll worry about that shit tomorrow; for now, I just want to hold her while I can, because something tells me when everything has a chance to settle in, it'll be the last time in a long time that she'll even be able to look at me.

Jori puts his arm around me and lets out a tired breath. The warmth of him against me is a comfort in a way and damaging in another, but I don't have it in my heart to turn him away. As his chest begins to steadily move up and down, and a small snore escapes him, I push my body back against his, molding myself into the safe place I've come to love being in for so many years.

I told him we'd be together and I meant it, but I don't know how much longer I can go on with this charade. It's not what he told me that's bothering me; rather, what he thinks he's hiding from me.

Where was he all day? Did he think of me, more than just the phone call? Is this something worth fighting for? When did everything go so fucking wrong?

I have more questions than answers right now, and it's fucking with me more than when I didn't know things were the way they are.

With as confused as I am about everything right now, I've also come to learn that I don't have any more tears for this situation. I'm saving those for Hoyt's last breath, if that day ever comes, but with Jori, I have none left.

I'm confusing him as much as I am myself, and I know it, but it's taking me more time to process things than I thought it would. I know that in the long run, I won't care, and I hope Jori knows that too.

Tomorrow, when we both wake up, I'll ask him where he was today. I'll ask him what he did and who he was with, and I'll sound like the jealous girlfriend I've committed myself to being.

And who knows?

Maybe, in the end, everything will be okay.

I reach underneath his arm and pull it closer as I close my eyes again. It took years for us to get to this point, and I'm not entirely sure if I'm ready to let it go just yet.

I'm hoping Hoyt can help me decide what the right thing to do is. I'm giving him another chance to be the father I can't really remember, and I know he won't let me down.

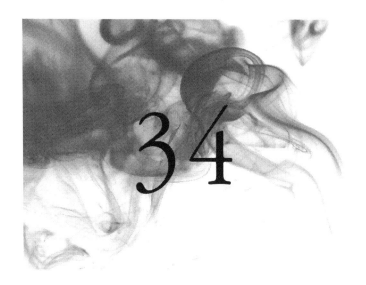

34

Mildred Mitchell-Bateman Hospital

5 years ago

I'm really nervous about getting caught right now, because I don't know what they'll do to—or with—me if they realize the documents I just handed them are fake. I paid a lot of money for them, and as long as I get to walk out of here with what I came for, it's money well spent.

The nurse at the front desk was really nice to me when I walked in and told her what I wanted.

She asked me for my paperwork, then told me to have a seat.

I've been sitting for about a fucking hour now, and she hasn't come back yet. No one has; it's almost like they forgot about me, and if someone doesn't tell me something soon, they might as well suit me up and toss me into a fucking room too.

It still makes me so damn angry that they took him like they did—kicking and screaming like a scared little boy, while Millie stood by with a smug look on her face, sucking on her fucking cigarette like she ever knew what was best for him.

I played a vicious game of tug of war with the men that came to take Jori away that day, but she held up some piece of paper saying Daddy had signed off on it. I never understood how he would be able to do something like that, since he's been in jail for so damn long, and finally realized she must have gone to see him. That, or she forged his fucking name.

Two can play at that game, I think as I nervously chew on my thumbnail.

That bitch will get what's coming to her one day, and I only hope I'm around to see it.

"Miss Blackburn?" I gasp at the sound of the nurse's voice and then giggle in embarrassment.

Getting to my feet, I walk over to the front desk and smile as brightly as I can, digging my nails into the counter so she can't see how hard I'm shaking. She smiles knowingly at me and for a moment, my heart stops beating.

"This place can get to you if you've never been in a hospital like this before," she says warmly. "I just wanted to let you know that they'll be bringing him up soon. They had to wait until he took his medication first."

My knees begin to shake in relief, and I feel faint. It worked—it fucking worked, and I'll be able to walk out of this place with Jori and he'll never have to come back again. I don't know how long until we'll be able to leave West Virginia, but I'll take him back to Harpers Ferry and start saving every nickel I can until I know we have enough to start over somewhere far away from all of this bullshit.

"So, if you'll just take a seat for a little while longer, I'll call you back up when he's on the floor," she says, sitting back down in her chair and signing the documents I gave her. I crane my neck slightly and can already see a pair of signatures on it, but I'll dissect the rest of that when I get it back.

For now, I just want him back with me, where he belongs.

As I sit down, I lean forward and prop my elbows up on my knees. It won't be long now, according to the nurse, but just how long is that really? Thirty minutes and an almost panic attack later, I get my answer.

"Miss Blackburn?"

I glance up at her and begin wringing my hands as she motions for me to come over to the desk. She smiles the same damn smile she's given me since I first walked into this godforsaken place, and hands me my manila folder.

"Everything is in order. He'll be escorted through that door in a moment," she says, pointing to a pair of doors on the other side of the reception desk.

"Can I …?" My voice trails off, but the hopeful-ness in my eyes is enough to finish my sentence for me.

"Of course, but you can't go near him until they hand him off to you, okay? We find that's a shock to our patients if they're suddenly confronted with a loved one before they have a chance to process it," she warns with a raised eyebrow.

I nod, walk over, and position myself so I know

I'll be the first thing he sees when he comes through the doors. I can hear a faint buzzing sound, followed by the mechanics of the doors slowly opening, and I take a deep breath.

I'm so hopeful right now that everything will be okay again, that I'm fighting the urge to just run through the doors and throw my arms around him.

But when he finally walks through the doors, my heart drops like a rock. His hair is disheveled, his lower lip is trembling, and his normally bright blue eyes are dull and red. He keeps his gaze on the floor, anger wrought all over his face, as two large orderlies hold him by either arm.

He cuts his eyes to either side of him and then looks up in confusion. I think he's starting to realize he's no longer in the back area of the facility where they've been housing him for the past year, and his breathing suddenly becomes erratic.

One of the large men motions for me to slowly walk forward, and as I do, Jori slowly raises his eyes. When they finally rest on me, his face crumples and he begins to sob.

"Are you gonna be okay if we let you go right now, Davidson?" the large man asks him gruffly.

He nods as he lets out another sob and the men move him forward, pushing him as gently as they can into my arms. His knees give way, and he wraps his arms around my waist as he cries. I can't remember a time I've ever seen him so distraught, and it makes me wonder just what the fuck exactly happened behind those secure double doors.

"On your feet," the man says, reaching for his arm, but I manage to smack his hand away with the folder.

"I'll take it from here," I reply coolly as a tear slips down my face. "He's not your property anymore."

Both men exchange a glance and the larger one shrugs and shakes his head as they both head back inside the facility. *Go fuck with the other loonies; this one is gonna be just fine.*

"Red," he manages to sob out, looking up at me. "You came to get me?"

I run a hand down the side of his face and nod. He buries his face in my stomach and cries harder than before.

"Come on; we've gotta get out of here. Once we're home, I'll fix you up a nice, warm bath, okay?" I say, trying my best to wrestle him to his feet. He's like dead weight right now, and it's hard for me to lift him without any help. It actually makes me wish I hadn't sassed the orderlies, 'cause they could have helped me.

"Jori? Come on. Get up," I say softly, as I give his shirt a tug. He takes a deep, shuddering breath before he finally pushes himself to his feet and leans his weight against me. I wrap an arm around his waist and do my best to walk him out of the facility without falling over.

I have no idea what the fuck they did to him in this place, and I won't ask. I only hope that after a few days, he'll be himself again, and if he isn't, I hope he can find a way to cope.

I won't medicate him—I refuse to force that bullshit into his body. He was just fine before Millie had him taken away, and he'll be just fine without it.

I'll do my best to take care of him, because no matter how much shit I've dealt with in my life, he's always found a way to take care of me.

When we get outside, he brings a hand up to his face to shield the sunlight, and takes a deep breath. I glance up at him and have to bite my lip to keep from crying again.

"Let's go home," I say to him softly, giving his side a squeeze.

Jori glances down at me, and for a moment, it seems like he's seeing me for the first time. A small smile creeps up the corner of his lips as he nods and pulls me into a hug.

"Thank you. Thank you, thank you," he whispers over and over into my ear.

It's amazing what freedom can do to a man—especially one who never deserved to be locked up to begin with. It's gonna take some time, but I'm willing to wait around for however long it takes for him to be himself again.

He'd do the same thing for me.

35

Present Day

I yawn widely when I wake up the next day. I'm pretty sure it's still morning, anyway, because the sliver of sunlight that managed to sneak into the room isn't as bright as it would be if it were midday.

When I feel Red's small body shift against me, my heart jumps into my throat. I wasn't expecting her to be on this bed with me when I woke up, and now I'm not sure if that's a good thing or if it's just gonna turn into another round of bullshit.

She turns on her side, her lips gently grazing my chest, and smiles. Her eyes are still closed, so I'm sure she's not aware of what she's doing, but it's starting to get me hard, so I move back from her a bit and place a hand gently on the side of her face.

"Morning," I say softly.

She cracks one eye open, smiles, and reaches for me, pulling herself against me again.

"Morning," she replies tiredly. She brings her small fist to her mouth as she yawns, then lowers it, snuggling back into my chest.

"Babe? Not a good idea right now," I say with a quiet chuckle, pulling myself away from her again.

"It's never been a bad idea before," she replies the smile still on her face as she reaches for me again. Only this time, she doesn't reach for my waist; this time, she reaches for my boxers and slides her hand into the fly, closing it around my dick, and I suck in my breath. I don't want to do this right now, because Christ knows if she's going to blow cold about it later, but I won't deny her, either.

She's had enough of that in her life.

I reach for her and pull her to me, wrapping my arms around her tightly as she begins to gently stroke me. I let out a content sigh as I place my chin on top of her head. Red's hands are fucking magic—they always have been—and her touch is the one thing that keeps me sane in this fucked up, miserable world.

I moan happily as she moves her hand faster, using her other hand to pull my boxers down.

"Oops," she giggles, when she gets tangled.

"I got it," I tell her with a smirk as she pulls her hand out of the fly and waits patiently.

I slide my thumbs into the waistband and pull them off. Once that's done, I toss them onto the floor and wrap my arms back around her as she grips my cock and resumes stroking me. My breath catches in my throat when she begins to move down the bed, her lips leaving a trail of soft kisses from my chest down to my stomach, and just above my dick. She's holding it firmly in her hand and looking up at me with her wide, inno-cent eyes, but the smile on her face right now is far from fucking innocent. It's the smile of a *very* naughty girl who knows what I like and isn't afraid to give it to me.

Red licks the tip of my cock and I take in a sharp breath. Her fucking mouth is even more magical than her hands, and I'm going to fucking freak out if she doesn't just go for it soon.

She tilts her head to the side and the smile turns into a devious grin. Using her other hand to get a firm grip on my balls, she suddenly sits up on her knees and gives me an unnerving stare.

"Where the fuck were you all day?" she asks in an even tone.

You've got to be fucking kidding me right now.

I groan and put my hands over my face for a moment, but when she tightens her grip and gives my balls a hard tug, I open them immediately and hold my hands up.

"Whoa there!" I say loudly. "Let's not rip those off."

"Where were you?" she asks again.

I should have known better by now that with the way shit has been recently, she would just roll over and fuck. Not that I've ever thought of her as that kind of girl, but it would have been nice right now.

"I went to Cold Spring," I say, reaching down and attempting to pry her hands off me.

Red shakes her head firmly and doesn't let go.

"I swear to God! That's where I was!" I say in a panic. At this point, I wouldn't put it past her to rip my balls off my body, and I'm frantically wracking my brain to figure out how to talk her out of it.

"Why did you smell like cigarettes last night then?" she asks in a low, even tone as she narrows her eyes.

"Because I went to Millie's! You know how much she fucking smokes. For fuck's sake, babe! Ease up a little down there," I plead, reaching for her hands again.

"Why?" she asks, digging her nails into my sack.

I let out a pained yell and grit my teeth. My eyes are watering, and I'm in danger of becoming a fucking eunuch here shortly, if she doesn't believe me.

"I went to tell her to stay out of our lives. Shit got out of hand, I ended up stomping her fucking throat in and she's in the trunk of the car," I confess in a rush.

Red finally pulls her hands away from me and I let out a long breath. I sit up as best I can and reach down to massage myself in an effort to dull some of the pain. She sits back on her heels, runs her hands irritably over her face, and sighs.

"Millie; check," she mutters glumly.

"What?" I ask her. The pain is starting to dull finally, and I'm regaining my bearings, but at least now I know never to leave for an entire fucking day and come back in the wee hours of the morning. It could mean my goddamn manhood.

"Millie, Doreen, Jake. The only one left at this point is Hoyt," she says with a heavy sigh as she attempts to push herself off the bed. But I'm faster than Red—much faster—and I grab her by the arms and pull her back up toward me.

"It's not like we have a fucking checklist," I grumble. "Millie was an accident. I lost my shit, and well …"

"I don't care about her," Red says, shaking her head vigorously. "I don't care about Jake, and I don't give a shit about Doreen, but Hoyt? I don't know, Jori; something's not right about what's happening to him."

I clear my throat and put an arm around her. Red falls against me and sighs heavily. To me, it really depends on how the situation is analyzed. The bastard threw me away because Doreen told him to; then, he had me fucking committed because Millie probably mooed at him one too many times, and he had the chance to turn me in but he didn't. What he's been through for the past fifteen years … what's waiting for him when he reaches the end of the road … as far as I'm concerned, he's fucking earned it. He knows it, and so do I. Why Red keeps pressing it is beyond me.

"Sorry about that," she says, running her hand over my stomach and looking up at me. "I just can't lose you too, you know? To anyone, for any reason."

"I'm not going anywhere, kid," I promise her. I gently lift her chin toward me and kiss her so softly that when a moan escapes her mouth, I smile.

"No. And you know why? 'Cause I just found out how dangerous you can be down there," I say with a chuckle.

"It won't hurt this time; I promise," she says, biting her lower lip.

"I don't trust you, babe," I reply with a shrug. "Besides, don't you wanna go out and do something today?"

Red pouts at me and I laugh. She's used to getting her way with that pout, but I'm still kind of scared for my balls right now, so I don't want her hands or mouth anywhere near them.

She arches her eyebrows at me. She's taking this as a challenge when it's absolutely not; however, when she reaches down and slides her panties off, I can't help but grin. Her pussy is far from dangerous with the exception of how addictive it is, and when she straddles me and reaches for my dick, I playfully slap her hand away and hold it up for her myself. She pushes me back against the headboard as she slides herself down onto it, and I lean my head back, letting out a breath.

Red arches her back slightly as she begins to gently rotate her hips, grinding into me, and it's in moments like this that I couldn't give two fucks what anyone thinks about us.

I grip one of her hips tightly and reach for her top with my free hand, but she beats me to it and pulls it off, tossing it at my face.

"Don't move." She leans forward to whisper in my ear. My cock is throbbing inside her warm, wet cunt, and I let out a throaty chuckle when she ties the shirt around my eyes. Red reaches for my hands and pushes them back against the headboard, holding them in place as she begins to grind her hips again.

She's depriving me of the honor of seeing and touching her, and it's so fucking maddening that I know I won't last much longer like this.

"Fuck, babe," I groan as I feel her tits pressing against me. She wants this more than I could have ever thought, and it makes me feel like shit may be okay again. Maybe not like it used to be, but close enough that I know she has no intention of leaving me.

"Faster, baby, please," I beg her. I can feel it building deep inside me, and I want to come inside her so bad right now that I'm grinding my teeth.

Red takes a deep breath and begins to bounce on my dick. She's not rotating her hips anymore; she's fucking *bouncing* on me, and I lean my head back, moaning louder than I ever have before.

"Don't fucking stop. Just like that," I half beg, half command her as my balls start tightening.

She lets out a sound that seems more like a whimper than a moan as she bounces harder, and in the next glorious moment, I let out a gasp as my cock finally drains inside her.

With a tired giggle, she falls against me, sweaty and breathing heavily. My hands are still firmly held in place, and as I try to steady my breathing, she leans her face up and kisses me gently on the nose before letting my hands go and undoing the makeshift blindfold.

"Do you love me?" she asks with a hopeful gaze in her eyes.

"More than anything," I reply, wrapping my

arms around her. She smiles as she climbs off me and I groan slightly, making a face. I always hated the way that felt, but I try not to make too big a deal about it. I don't want her to think she's ever done anything wrong, because in all honesty, we can't be stuck together—no matter how lovely the sentiment may seem.

"Go take a shower, Davidson. You smell like pussy and sweat; it reminds me of that guard in the facility," she says with a chuckle.

I roll my eyes as I watch her pull her panties on and walk over to sit in the chair by the window. She pulls the curtain back slightly and sighs.

And just like that, it looks like we're back to cold again.

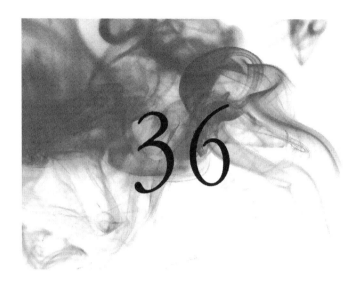

36

I sigh as I pull my legs underneath myself in the chair. I don't know if I should tell Jori that Hoyt called while he was gone, because I don't know how he'll react. He'll probably wonder how he knew where we were staying to begin with, but that's a little bit of information I slipped to Officer Davis the last time I was up at the prison. I told him that if Hoyt felt the need to talk, he could call me here and I'd gladly reimburse the hotel for the charges.

I shouldn't keep it a secret, because Hoyt told me he wants to see the both of us. He begged for just one more visit before it's all said and done, which leads me to believe he's got his date now.

It's been a day or two since I've been up to see him, and I think our visits have been doing more harm than good. When he sees me, he sees his failures instead of all the wonderful moments we' had before Doreen died.

I'm not the saving grace I thought I would be— I'm the damnable grace that's pushed him to want to die faster than he should.

And for what? There's no sin he's committed that needs atoning for. Was he a great father? No, but he damn sure tried his best, and I can forgive him for the nights I spent alone with Doreen. I can forgive him for all the things Jake did to me, and the hatred Millie poured all over me like molten lava; what I can't forgive him for is dying with a final secret I know is just on the tip of his tongue.

The door to the bathroom opens and I glance over to find Jori standing in the doorway, one hand propped up on the door frame, eyeing me with a look of concern and confusion.

"Can I ask you something?" he says quietly.

I start chewing on my thumbnail and nod. Now is not the time for riddles or candor, but I can that something is bothering the fuck out of him. It's just up to him if he wants to really say what it is.

"Alright," he says, running a hand back through his damp hair. He shifts uncomfortably, securing the towel around his waist, before he crosses his arms and looks at me with serious eyes. "Do you think your life would be better with Hoyt? Instead of with me, I mean."

I let out a sigh as I drop my hand onto my leg and shake my head. 'I don't know. I was never given the chance to try you both on for size, you know?"

He looks away for a moment as he nods, but then turns his eyes back to me because he knows there's more I need to say on this matter.

"If you want me to be honest, I would have liked the chance to get to know Hoyt more than I do. I would have loved to have had a happy, normal family life, but that wasn't in the cards for me—for either of us. What I have now, with you, makes up for every night I didn't get tucked into bed by Hoyt. It makes up for every scraped knee he didn't get to kiss, and it makes up for all the love I was never able to experience with him. I won't choose, Jori. I'll never be able to do that truthfully, because I just don't know."

He clears his throat and runs a hand over his face. It's not the answer he wanted—it was the truth, and the truth fucking sucks.

He walks over to me and crouches next to my chair, resting a hand on my thigh.

"If you want more time with Hoyt, I can give it to you. I just need to know," he says softly, a sad smile adorning his face.

I let out a chuckle. "Hoyt Blackburn doesn't have any time left, and there's nothing either of us can do about it."

"But what if there was? Something we could do about it?" he presses quietly.

I turn my eyes toward him. He looks so lost right now and it reminds me of when I sprung him from the mental facility. I smile sadly and shake my head. "I love my father. I know that sounds insane with all the shit that's gone on, but it's the truth. I've also learned to live without him; you, I've had by my side through every scraped knee, every foul touch, and every tear I felt would drown me in my sleep. I can't live without you, Jori."

His lower lip begins to tremble and his eyes water dangerously. "Red, I have to tell you something."

"Hoyt called while you were gone," I say,

cutting him off. "He wants to see us tomorrow night, and I told him we'd be there."

Jori pulls his hand away from my leg, stands up, and with a heavy sigh, nods. He knows as much as I do that this means it's the end of the line for Hoyt Blackburn, but I wonder if his sigh is sorrow for the father he never knew, or the man he helped condemn.

Jori Davidson doesn't have any more secrets he can hide from me. Hoyt told me everything on the phone call, but what neither of them were aware of was that I already knew the truth. I played the part of the shocked daughter when he told me, and I think I did my job well.

"Go take care of the trunk problem after you get dressed, please. The last thing we need to take to a maximum security prison is another dead relative when they're planning on handing us one soon, anyway," I say to him quietly before he walks into the bathroom and closes the door.

Pushing the curtain aside again, I look out into the sky and wonder if I'm doing the right thing. I hate to think it, but I can only hope I'm making the right choice in letting Hoyt die for a crime he didn't commit.

37

Sing Sing Correctional Facility
12 Hours To Go

I smile when my kids walk into the room the prison has given us. I haven't been able to sit down, so I've been leaning on the back of the chair waiting for them, and when Gracie walks in, I hold my arms out. She comes over immediately and hugs me, taking in a deep breath and I hope the smell is something she'll be able to remember for the rest of her life. Maybe they'll let me give her one of my shirts I haven't washed yet. I just want her to have something to remember me by that might make her smile instead of think of all the bad times.

"Hi baby," I whisper into her ear, hugging her tightly.

"Hi Daddy," she replies into my chest. I close my eyes for a moment and let myself linger in the sweet sound of her calling me Daddy for what may be the last time. I bite my lip so I don't cry—she needs me to be strong right now, and that's how I plan on letting her remember me.

Gracie finally pulls away from me and glances over her shoulder. We both look at Jori, who's standing on the other side of the table, his hands drumming the back of the chair he's leaning against as he eyes us hugging each other.

"Hey," I say, holding out an outstretched hand toward him.

He turns his face away for a moment, grinding his teeth together, before he lets go of the chair and crosses his arms over his shoulder.

A nod is what he gives me in the place of a handshake, and even though it's not what I wanted, it's better than nothing.

"Hoyt," he says, rocking side to side.

I look down at Gracie, who's stiffened in my arms, and shrug. "Let's sit down and talk for a bit."

I reach forward and pull out a chair for her, then take the one next to her. I glance over at Jori and nod at the chair he had been standing behind, but he just scoffs and continues rocking.

"Sit down," Gracie hisses at him angrily.

He gives her a dirty look but complies, and it makes me chuckle. Big, bad Jori Davidson, who managed to scare most of the adults in his life, listens to the one person he could never say no to.

Which reminds me.

"How are you two getting along these days?" I ask, resting my elbows on the table and looking at Gracie. She'll tell me the truth, whereas Jori will lie and say what he thinks I want to hear. I didn't tell Gracie he's her blood yet, because I'm hoping he's been man enough to do that himself already.

"Good," Gracie says with a nod. "Good days, bad days, but mostly good."

"I'm glad to hear that," I reply, giving her arm a squeeze. She smiles at me and glances at Jori who's watching us with contempt. That boy never could learn to love anyone who wasn't Gracie, and while that should be okay, the way he chooses to love her is not.

"What do you guys like to do together?" I ask, smiling at my baby.

"Fuck," Jori replies.

Gracie's mouth drops slightly open as I sit up in my chair and look at him in disbelief. *He didn't tell her.*

"Jori if you can't be a rational adult right now, you can sit there with your mouth shut," she snaps at him.

I want to get out of my chair and slap him. I want to smash his face against the fucking wall and scream some sense into him, but he's so far gone at this point that he'll never see reason. If anything, he just wants to get a rise out of me because he thinks I abandoned him, when that's far from the truth.

"It's okay, Gracie," I say to her quietly, my eyes still on Jori. "He never could understand reason … Always lost in a world of his own and refusing to come out of it."

Jori arches an eyebrow at me before he turns his face away and laughs.

"And that concludes family time. Come on," he says, getting to his feet and holding out a hand to Gracie.

"No," she replies softly. "I'm not leaving until I

have to. And neither are you, so please sit back down and just listen, if you can't participate responsibly. It may answer the question you asked me yesterday."

Jori looks at her and I can see his eyes starting to water. Whatever this question is must have been of some importance to him if it's getting that kind of reaction right now.

"Yeah, okay," he says quietly, sitting back down in the chair. "Sorry about that."

"It's alright, son," I reply evenly.

He cuts his eyes nervously toward Gracie, but she's too busy picking at her fingernails to notice.

"Wait, I have an idea. Why don't you two get closer, and I'll take some pictures," he says, reaching into his side pocket. I raise an eyebrow and wonder how it's possible for him to go from such a clusterfuck of a soul to doing something so damn heartwarming.

"Sneak it in, huh?" I ask him with a grin.

Jori shrugs and nods. "Yeah. Fuck it. It's mine, and they can't take it away from me. Alright, here we go."

He gets to his feet as I put an arm around Gracie and pull her close. She rests her head on the side of my face and when Jori tells us to smile, I can hear a small whimper escape her.

"Don't cry, baby. It's just how things have to go," I whisper, giving her arm a squeeze. She reaches up a hand to wipe away her tears before grabbing mine and taking a steadying breath.

"Wow. If only you two knew how much alike you really look," he remarks, looking at the picture on his phone. "Let's do another one. Try to smile this time, Red. You grimaced in the last one."

Gracie laughs despite herself, and takes another breath when Jori tells us to smile.

"Cool," he says with a nod, looking at the pictures.

"Now you two," she says, surprising us both by getting to her feet and taking the phone from him.

"Um—"

"Go," she says, wiping away a tear and giving Jori a gentle shove in my direction.

"It's alright, baby. He doesn't have to if he doesn't want to," I say with a wave.

"No. I really want this picture. I remember how he used to look at you when we were kids, Daddy. He may not be able to admit it now, but you're still his hero, and I'd like to be able to have a picture of the only two men who ever gave a shit about me together. Now get up and smile."

With a chuckle, I get to my feet as Jori comes over to stand next to me. "She always this bossy?" I ask him good-naturedly.

"She's a chick—of course she is," he replies with a wry smile.

I grin at him and for just the slightest moment, I can see his eyes soften. It doesn't last longer than a second though, as he coughs and crosses his arms over his chest.

"That's a shit ton of tattoos," I remark, still grinning.

"Yeah. I got bored. Alright, look at the tiny chick in the room, she's waiting on us," he says, nodding toward Gracie.

"Smile," she says softly as she holds up his phone. I don't know what comes over me—if it's the instinct to be his father for the first time in my life, or just having my only son this close to me, but I reach over and put an arm around his shoulder and smile proudly at Gracie.

Jori stiffens slightly but relaxes under the weight of my hand. At this point, if he tried to resist, I'd probably smack him around. I'm scheduled to die in the morning anyway, so it's not like I have anything to lose.

Gracie looks down at the phone and smiles, before she wipes away yet another tear and walks toward us.

"Um, you're the tallest, you do it," she says, handing me the phone.

"Fuck if I know how to use one of these things, Gracie," I reply with a nervous laugh.

"Just hold it up, and you see that circle? When we're all smiling at that little camera hole up there, press it," she says, wrapping her arms around my waist. I do as I'm told and when Jori leans into the picture stone-faced, Gracie ribs him. He rolls his eyes and sighs but manages to spare a smile for his old man, and I get the picture I've been wanting for twenty-seven years.

Me, my daughter, and my son.

Smiling and together without the devil that was Doreen impeding on my chance to be a father to both of them instead of just one.

When I hear the door start to slide open, I quickly shove the phone back to Jori, who slips it into his pocket.

Davis walks in somberly and sighs.

"It's time to go, kids," he says to us quietly. "Say your good-byes."

"Thanks, man," I say to him. He nods and tells us he'll be waiting outside the door.

Gracie turns to face me and her face crumples. She immediately begins to sob as she wraps her arms around my shoulders, and I have to take the deepest breath I can muster to hold back my own feelings of regret and sorrow.

"I'm so sorry, Daddy," she wails into my chest. "It shouldn't be like this; it shouldn't!"

Jori reaches over and puts a hand on her shoulder. She turns her face slightly to look at him, and I can see the weight of the world crushing his soul right now.

"I'll take care of it," he says to her softly. Jori reaches for Gracie, takes her face in his hands, and looks at her for a moment before he leans down and kisses her. But it's not the way a brother should kiss his sister, and it makes me so sick to my fucking stomach right now.

And even still, if he's gonna do what I think he's gonna do, I won't allow it to happen.

"Take her and go. I'll be okay," I say, pulling Gracie's arms away from me and handing her over to Jori. He looks over at me in disbelief, his lower lip trembling, and sadness in his eyes.

"Hoyt—" he says, shaking his head.

"Take care of my Gracie for me. I never got the chance to, and I'm asking you to do that as a favor for me," I say, shaking my head and putting my hands on my hips. "You kids get out of here. I'll see you tomorrow, and then who knows when."

Gracie is a sobbing mess in her brother's arms, and he does the one thing I wanted from the moment I walked in. Jori looks at me, extends his hand, and takes mine firmly in his.

"I'm sorry," he says softly as a tear spills down his cheek.

"Time's up," Davis calls from the doorway.

I smile at them as best I can, and watch as he leads her to the door. Once they disappear, I collapse into my chair and begin to cry.

I failed her again.

I should have told her Jori isn't the man she should end up with, but I just couldn't crush her again.

I've done that enough.

Sing Sing Correctional Facility
The Death House, 6:37 AM

I always thought that when I grew up, I would have the proverbial American Dream. A house, a wife, and two kids—a boy and a girl.

But as I walk toward the death chamber with Davis on one side of me and Morgan on the other, a priest leading the way, I wonder how it all turned into a fucking nightmare instead.

I'm not afraid to die; fuck, it'll be the most exciting thing I've done in years. I'm just afraid of leaving Gracie and Jori behind without a hand to guide them, because Millie has been useless since she was a fucking kid. Hopefully, she won't give them too much trouble, and maybe she'll keep her fucking mouth shut about them being blood. That's Jori's place to tell Gracie, and those will be his lumps to take when it finally sinks in with her.

That's the thing about my baby girl—it always took her longer than usual to realize things and understand what was going on around her, but she's never been given the chance to be her own person, 'cause there was always someone bossing her the fuck around when I wasn't looking.

"Hey, I appreciate it and all, but can you knock it off?" I call out to the priest. He turns around to look at me and nods, closing his Bible, and leading the rest of the way silently.

The only sounds in the hallway now are my chains clanging around, and I smile. I get why it's called the Last Mile now. It seems like it takes an eternity to get to your destination, only to be sent on to eternity itself.

I glance over at Davis when I hear him sniffle, but he turns his face away. I like him—I always did. He may have been a hard ass when I first got here,

THE LIES BETWEEN US

but that's because it's his job; however, we've grown to be great friends over time.

"Chin up, Davis. I'll be out of your hair soon," I joke softly.

He looks at me, red-faced and misty-eyed, and offers a small smile.

"Just do me that favor I asked of you, alright" I remind him quietly. He nods and puts his hand on my shoulder as the door finally begins to loom closer.

I stop walking for a moment and the C.Os tighten their grips on my arms.

"I'm not gonna give you any trouble," I say to them quietly. "I just think it's insane how this is the last time I'll ever do something as simple as walk through a door."

"I'm sorry, Hoyt," Davis says softly, before he gives my arm a tug. I smile up at him and shake my head. "I've heard that enough times in my life," I reply with a chuckle. "Let's just get this over with."

When we finally reach the door, Morgan lets go of my arm as he unlocks it with one of the many keys on his key-ring and pushes it open. I step inside and raise an eyebrow when I see the table. It's weird; I expected it to be much grander than it is, but it's really nothing more than a cot with an extension for each of my arms.

Davis reaches down and starts to uncuff me and remove my chains, before grabbing my elbow and walking me over to the table. I shake my head and scoff, putting my hands on my hips for a moment.

And then I climb on and lie down in direct correlation with the way the cot is shaped, and wait. A man in a white coat steps forward and wraps a plastic tube around my arm, then slaps around the exposed flesh until he finds a vein. I raise my head slightly and watch him slide a needle in, hook it up to a tube, then step back.

The Warden walks into the room a few seconds later, hovers over me, and puts a hand on my shoulder.

"You're a good man, Hoyt Blackburn. I'm gonna miss talking to you," he says quietly before he takes his place next to the doctor and nods.

Morgan moves toward the small circle of curtains that were blocking the windows to another room, and I lean my head back down and sigh.

They have me strapped in and ready to go. I'm not a martyr though; I'm just a simple man trying to do the right thing, hoping it'll knock some sense into his kids one day.

I hear a loud wail come from the other side of the window, and I turn my head toward the sound. I smile sadly when I see Gracie sitting with her face in her hands, sobbing hysterically. Jori's sitting next to her, half slumped in his chair, his legs stretched out in front of him, arms crossed over his chest. I used to see that look on his face a lot when I would go visit him at Millie's, and I can't help but wonder if maybe I had just told him I was his father, things would have been different.

Other than my babies, there are a few other faces I don't know, so I turn my eyes back toward the ceiling. Davis moves a microphone over my face, and the Warden asks me if I want to make a last statement.

I wasn't ready for this, because I don't think anything I could say now would make any kind of statement that would affect the lives that are so irrevocably broken already.

"Um, I just want to tell Gracie that I love her, and that I'm sorry. And I want Jori to know that I love him too, and I'm counting on him to take care of Gracie for me. That's it," I say, leaning my head back down and closing my eyes.

"Goddammit," I hear Davis mumble when the Warden gives the order. I hear the machine turn on, but I keep my eyes closed. There's nothing left worth seeing in this world, and I'd rather take the images I've had in my heart for years now into the unknown.

A happy little Gracie playing outside with a happy young man she never knew was connected to her in more ways than one.

Good-bye, my beautiful babies.

39

The Long Road Home
Present Day

"You okay?"

Jori squeezes my hand reassuringly and I sigh. It's a question I have to analyze over and over again, because I honestly don't know how to answer it. Hoyt is dead for a crime he didn't commit, and we're on our way back to Harpers Ferry like it's just another fucking day.

"I don't know," I reply quietly. I lean my forehead against the cool glass of the window and watch Ossining go by in a blur of emotion and dead hopes. I'll come back for his ashes, but for now, I have to get out of this godforsaken fucking town. I take a deep breath of the white shirt that still bears his scent, and gently rub it against my nose, before I lower it back to my lap.

Hoyt's death had no effect on Jori, other than a few shed tears, a sniffle, and a complete disregard for what we were watching. Once Hoyt's chest finally became dormant, Jori put an arm around me and held me close while I sobbed. To be honest, I don't think I was crying for the man on the table, but rather for the man who did his best in a failed attempt to provide a stable home in a horribly turbulent environment.

My father died a long time ago, so I can't really say I knew the man who gasped his last breaths in front of our eyes.

Maybe it will all make sense one day, for now, it's just another dead relative in a world they never had a chance in.

"Have you decided yet?" he asks me softly.

I can tell by the tone of his voice that he knows that now isn't the time to ask me this question, yet he needs the answer as much as I do.

"Can we talk about this when we get home, please?" I ask, glancing at him tiredly.

Jori nods as he lifts my hand to his lips and kisses it so gently that a shiver runs through my body. He clears his throat as he lowers my hand back down and shifts uncomfortably in his seat. I watch him curiously as he steals a glance in the rear-view mirror, before squeezing my hand again.

He still thinks he has secrets he's keeping from me—that if, or when, he decides to tell me what really happened to Doreen, it will be a deal breaker —but he doesn't know that I was there that night. Watching him in amazement, wonder, and all of the beautiful and ugly things I shouldn't have felt while he beat the life out of her.

I sigh as I think of how I snuck out of Uncle Jake's house when I was sure he had finally gone to sleep. I opened the window and climbed down, using the tree that sat just outside of it like Jori had taught me to do so many times before.

I ran all the way home, barefoot and carefree, because I would be with my daddy that night and not have to worry about anyone touching me in any way they had no right to. And I just knew in my heart that Jori would come get me like he always did—a young, cold-hearted knight in shining armor that only ever saw hope when he looked into my eyes.

He's fidgeting in his chair next to me, which makes me a little concerned about getting back to Harpers Ferry in one piece.

"Pull over at the next rest area," I say tiredly. No more games, no more secrets, and no more hiding things that have come to light so many years ago. We're going to have it out, and maybe then I'll know what the fuck I want to do with this.

"You gotta go?" he asks with a nervous smile.

"Something like that," I reply, squeezing his hand.

Jori nods and clears his throat as he drives. Another twenty miles pass before I point out a sign and he switches lanes. A few moments later, he's pulling into an empty spot in front of a small, brick building, and I pull my hand away from him.

"Get out of the car," I tell him softly as I push my door open and step out. I stole a glance at his face as I exited, and the look of confusion is as prominent now he's walking around toward me as it was at my request.

"May I have the keys please?" I ask, holding out a hand.

"Why?" he asks, furrowing his brow.

"Because I want you to listen to me, Jori," I reply simply.

He lets out a laugh as he crosses his arms over his chest, and clutches the keys tightly in his hand. "Nah. I don't think I'm going to wanna hear what you have to say."

"What have I ever asked you for?" I say to him. shaking my head. "I won't say what I have to until you give me those keys and you can wander around the rest of your life wondering what I *could* have said to you today, instead of what I *did*."

He shakes his head as he gives in and hands me the keys. Jori leans on the hood of the car and slides his hands in his pocket before he shrugs. "Okay, so what's the fucking problem, Red?"

I put my hands on my hips, the keys dangling from my partially closed fist, and tilt my head.

"Are we done playing this damn game now? We got what we wanted, didn't we?" I ask him tiredly. I have a headache that's growing by the second, and it's due to nothing more than the angry little boy sitting in front of me, instead of the man I know is inside somewhere.

"What are you talking about?" he asks gruffly before spitting on the pavement.

"Do you have anything you need to tell me?" I shoot back at him evenly.

"No."

"You're lying," I reply through gritted teeth. "I'm not a fucking child anymore, so stop trying to protect me, and just tell me the truth."

He clenches his teeth and his jaw squares tightly. His eyebrows are arched, but his face is overshadowed by anger and I know he's trying his hardest to stay calm.

"Get angry!" I shout at him, lifting my arms in the air. "If that's what it fucking takes for you to tell me what you think I don't already know, then get angry!"

"Lower your fucking voice, *Gracie,*" he commands through gritted teeth. He puts the emphasis on my name to let me know this is a situation he's trying to defuse before he loses his shit, but I want him to. I want him to get so angry he can't stand it, because that's when he's at his most honest.

"Tell me what happened to Doreen," I say, crossing my arms again. "And tell me the truth."

Jori scoffs and looks away for a moment before he gets to his feet. "Alright. You wanna know what happened to Doreen? She got her fucking skull caved in. She didn't even see it coming, and she probably choked to death on her own fucking blood, and I don't give one good goddamn that she's dead," he finishes with a shout.

A young couple walking by with two small children eye us warily, and Jori turns his face toward the sky. I can tell he wants to keep going, and while I want nothing more than to hear him out right now, I don't want anyone else to.

"Hold on," I say to him quietly. "Can we help you?" The young man puts his arms around his gal and pulls her along, as she pushes the kids ahead. "Fucking nosy bastards," I mutter, keeping my eyes on them until they get into their car and back out. Once their car is driving away back toward the freeway, I turn my attention back to Jori and nod.

"Hoyt didn't kill her. I did," he says quietly, giving me a level stare.

"I know."

Jori blinks rapidly a few times and his gaze turns from hard to confused He shakes his head and walks slowly in a circle, before he bends over and grips his knees with his hands.

"What did you say?" he asks shakily.

"I said, I know," I repeat. Jori looks up at me and stands to his full height, his lower lip trembling dangerously. His eyes are brimming with tears, but for which emotion, I'm not sure.

"How?"

"Sit down, I want to tell you a story," I say quietly. He turns around and walks two steps back toward his car before he props himself back up on the hood again. I chew the inside of my cheek before I run a hand back through my hair and look him in the eye. "The night Doreen died, Hoyt had dropped me off at Millie's. You weren't home yet, and she took the opportunity to browbeat me into leaving. I went to Jake's, because that was the only place close enough for me to get to at the time. Anyway," I say with a sigh, "I could tell he was gonna start with his handsy bullshit at some point, so I barricaded myself in his room when I was given the chance. I waited until he fell asleep, and then I climbed out the window like you taught me to." I walk over and scoot him to the side so that I can sit next to him. "I ran all the way home. I was so happy because I would be in the same house with Hoyt, and I knew you'd come get me at some point, and we'd go off into the tree house and sleep like we always used to, you know? I crept up to my room while they were arguing, and I think I fell asleep at some point because I remember jumping at the sound of Hoyt's voice. He was yelling in a panic, and I crept down the stairs to see what the hell was going on. That's when I saw you," I say quietly, a sad smile on my face. "I saw Hoyt shaking you, asking you what you had done, and then telling you to leave. I know you killed Doreen, because Hoyt told me as much that night, but I guess I just didn't care, because the nightmare was finally over, you know?"

"Wow," he says, still looking down at his feet. He shifts for a moment to cross his legs, and I lean my head on his shoulder. His way of calming me down is a gentle kiss and a soft touch; my way of calming *him* down is by placing my head on his shoulder. It's a small gesture to let him know I still care about him no matter what, and it's usually well received.

"So as you can see, nothing you have to tell me will make me turn away from you. I just don't like the secrets and the lies." I finish with a shrug. "We're better than that."

"What did you mean when you said we got what we wanted?" he asks, turning his head toward me. His lips graze my forehead and I close my eyes to take in the moment, before I get to my feet and drape my arms around his shoulders.

"Doreen is dead. Jake is dead. Millie is dead. Hoyt's dead too, and even though he really didn't deserve it, he kind of did for picking one of us over the other. If you think about it, it's kind of like checking off items on a grocery list—even though you insisted we don't have one—and because they're dead, we finally get to *live.*"

"How?" he asks, putting his hands on my forearms.

"Together," I reply in confusion.

"Together, *how?*" he presses, moving his lips to my hand. "You still haven't given me a solid answer on that."

I smile and lean close enough to feel his breath on my face. He closes his eyes and turns his head so his lips are now on the side of my face, and I suddenly find myself wondering what the world will think of us.

A pair of sinners bound by blood, hiding in plain sight from a wicked world that doesn't deserve something as pure as what we have. Wrong or right, this is the man I love, and there's no one left to stand in our way.

I'll grieve my father for a few more days, and

I'll put his ashes on a mantle in the living room, but other than that, I have everything I could ever want, and it's hidden behind the eyes of the man with the beautiful, bitter blue eyes that only ever wanted someone to love him.

And he chose me.

ABOUT THE AUTHOR

Yolanda Olson is an award-winning and international bestselling author. Born and raised in Bridgeport, CT where she currently resides, she usually spends her time watching her favorite channel, Investigation Discovery. Occasionally, she takes a break to write books and test the limits of her mind. Also an avid horror movie fan, she likes to incorporate dark elements into the majority of her books.

You can keep in touch with her on Facebook, Twitter, and Instagram.

facebook.com/yolandasendlesswords

twitter.com/symphonyyolanda

instagram.com/ihateyolandaolson

goodreads.com/RoxXie13ells

27734619R00196

Made in the USA
Columbia, SC
28 September 2018